Gas Station Divas

By Leslie Jones McCloud
Copyright 2005

Bumpkin:
Gas Station Divas Prologue

Fatalistic, dramatic, labile, saccharine: everyone loved Marion. She loved that everyone currently in her world, loved her and wanted the best for her as it was not always that way. Not being one to dwell in the past, Marion would occasionally put her path under review as to keep perspective. She wanted to examine her own thoughts, making sure not to make the same mistakes twice or eight times. Being stuck in a Groundhog Day scenario was a fear. Going in circles was not an activity she sought and silently rebuked those who did engage.

Marion did her best thinking in a hot bubble bath of handcrafted products and on the toilet. Today, she reviewed her thoughts while being hooked up to a colonic machine, situated in a trendy Chicago south side neighborhood. Marion preferred operating outside of where she lived, as to go unnoticed.

The stifling heat of the room perforated her periodic thought review of lessons learned and dotted her forehead with sweat. Marion began to regret the three bags of Brazilian wavy she asked her beautician, Angela, to sew into her hair. Marion was still getting used to having a full salary and was spending like crazy on all of the indulgences she had always wanted for herself and the kids. The hair was beautiful but it was voluminous.

She sat still for the procedure because she had no choice as she was literally tethered to a machine. Struggling against that tube up her rump would only prolong the procedure.

Marion had been plagued by constipation as far back as she could remember. Lying on the table, she recalled her mother administering Castoria on demand as Marion was filled with bowel tightening anxieties even as a little girl. Marion would hold her bowels for hours, dancing around, squeezing it up to hold it in and finally pushing, pushing, pushing it out. Having had missed several opportunities to go, the simple, natural process was made nightmarish.

Even back then Marion thought, she had control issues. While rich girls were starving themselves thin, Marion was eating everything in sight and then holding her bowels. It never helped her natural apple shape and always embarrassed her mother. Marion was weird. Her mother never knew what to do about it so she ignored it and gave her the medicinal, sweet-tasting brown liquid. As an adult, her husband's cousin's wife turned her on to Senna leaf tea. Marion's bowels were so messed up after that on again, off again relationship that she had to keep her colonic appointments. She figured she might as well look good while laying draped upon a table with a tube up her rump. She never wanted to see the business travel down that tube. She found that vulgar.

The job Marion had was hectic but easy. Making things up for a living is how her mom characterized what she got paid very well to do. It was partially correct. She invented many, many scenarios to conceal the inner workings of Durable Medical Supply. It was the only corporation of note in her town. It employed lots of locals but the top jobs usually went to more worldly people. Although she was native to Indiana, she rarely traveled outside her circle of life-long friends and spent little time interacting with the people so to speak, so it was really as if she wasn't from there. She had none of the tell-tale ways that would indicate she was raised in an

4

urban setting. She often had to convince people of the high school she attended. She had to recall the people she grew up hearing about and what was going on back in the day.

It was tedious but it was a face she had to put on. Getting people who really cared very little about what she what she had to say, to pay attention to her long enough to get her point across, was a tiresome affair. Strangely, people knew enough about her to know about her divorce. Her husband remarried fairly quickly telling her he did not want to be alone. She thought it strange of him to want to remain legally married but remain physically and emotionally apart so she opted for divorce. Little did she know he would fall dead of a heart attack five years later. His widow put him away nicely. There were plenty of flowers and wreaths but none of his many girlfriends.

Willard left his bride after finding she could not bear children due to her weight, according to their fertility specialist. Willard kept as a concubine, a woman with three little boys. He courted three other women—none of whom were allowed to attend the wake or the funeral or the repass. Marion was allowed in the front pew. She was inconsolable but comforted by her good friend Toni, who felt sorry for her. It was pitiful. The children were confused about the entire event and their mother was temporarily insane and remained so until her own mother removed her to the Escalade for a wild, screaming and crying ride home.

All he had to do was move to Florida, Marion thought to herself, and life would have been good for all of them. His wife was on board, hoping the move would help him to break ties with his other women. He'd still be alive if he had only agreed to move to Florida to help with the kids. Willard was a magic man as he could find a job anywhere. He was the make-something-out-of-nothing king which is why she married him initially. He asked Marion several times while she still had a modest bump, to get a quickie wedding but Marion, thinking she was being modern, opted for the bumpkin route and remained unmarried until much later. Willard was raised to have a certain set of manners and ways, like most who were raised upper class. He loved Marion and waited until she decided to marry eight years later. She had actually spent over half her life with him as they met and married young. But now, he was gone. Willard was the only one who understood her hopes and desires for a career and a good purposeful life. She thought Willard indestructible. She thought he'd be there forever but he was gone and she was alone.

"All done." the woman said, gentle with the tube as she slid it out of Marion's rump.

Marion lay there for a while to gather herself as she had gotten teary eyed thinking about her situation and Willard. It had been six years and his death still affected her greatly. She also lay on the table because she always felt so filthy after the colonic. The lubricant used to ease the tube inside her rump, gave her already jelly butt an unusual and slippery feel that she just had to eradicate before leaving and sitting on a towel on the drive home. She could not tolerate both the butt lube and the towel. Making matters worse but better, is that Marion opted for the oil colonic this time so she was sure to be leaking all over everywhere, all evening long. It would be a long night of staying in with wine and vodka and kids. The kids never understood mommy's nasty, slippery butt issues or her need to sit on a towel. They smartly did not want to know about it, either.

Marion created a low stress environment for her children. She did not want them growing up with free floating anxieties and laxatives and worries over everything as she did when she was little. She felt it too much for kids to be brought up that way with all of the yelling and emotions and such. Turns out her parent's way was better because while her kids did not exhibit signs of anxiety or bowel holding, they gave her hell and heaps more anxiety with all of the whining and crying and cussing and the beating up of her furniture. As her son grew, she understood why no one ever wanted to rent to people with kids. Kids are destructive little noise makers. However, being the indulgent parent, Marion quietly replaced the broken chairs and then smothered her children with love until they quieted down, even if it was just to avoid cloying mommy. Because she didn't yell much, when she did kick up a fuss it didn't take much to get the kids in line.

If her mom, Cleo, knew she was spending $75 a session to get a tube of oil pumped up her rump, Marion would lose all credibility at the monthly prayer meetings held at her aunt's house. Mom would not keep that secret. Marion shut down her thought review as she untied the sash on her gown, slid off of the table and got into her street clothes. She knew to wear dark sweats to colonic appointments— nothing form-fitting and no undies. The outfit would go directly into the wash the moment she stepped into her condo. Then, Marion would put on an even ragged pair of sweats to leak onto. She thought about changing her diet as to avoid the colonics but decided not to add yet another task to her to-do list. A separate meal plan for her on top of cooking for the kids would not be a good idea. She was already chronically tired unless she went to the gym and took her vitamins. Her schedule was already crowded enough.

Marion lit a cigarette as soon as she slid into her leather seats. They smelled so luxurious. Her drop top powder blue Lexus was purchased used and fully loaded. She and the kids kept it a mess but it was hers outright. It really wasn't a car for a mommy of two but for a single woman, as her parents pointed out after the purchase. The chiding never stops, Marion thought to herself as she punched buttons on the radio and thumped ashes at the same time. Although she had on dark sweats, she still wore high wedge Sketchers with it to dress it up. She figured why should she look completely bad while out. She even wore her gold ankle chain. The hair sucked even more age from her already youthful face. If she could only work off that pot belly.

Marion inherited the figure of her grandmother. It was not the young, pretty, thin-waisted, red lipstick wearing version of her grandmother who she never really got to know except through photographs but the retired and I'm done, grandmother who babysat all of her grandkids.

Mae was still a firecracker even at 87. Mae's father, Marion's great-grandfather, was said to pass for White. Some folks call it Creole but being the bumpkins they were, they still called it passing, like folks down south. Granny was fairly light, like coffee with too much cream in it.

Marion thought it remarkable that Big Momma, Granny's mother, was the color of ebony and Granny the color of pale. It was almost as if they weren't related. It wasn't until Mae's daughters had put her in a nursing home, did Marion notice just how pale and thin Granny really was. Her skin was thin and very white—so white Marion could see the blue of her veins running up her arms. Marion wondered how she had not noticed such a difference before but Granny loved the outdoors and barbequing so Marion never much saw her grandmother without a tan.

It didn't help that Granny's children whispered about how Big Momma had to run away with Grandpa (as they were chased out of the south) and left Granny behind, down south, to be raised by her grandmother. It also didn't help matters that their Grandpa died fairly young, leaving Big Momma alone. Granny looked out for Big Momma over the years because that is what children do but there were still lingering mother/daughter tensions over unresolved issues.

Granny, being self-reliant, had practically re-built a house for herself and her youngest daughter who still lived with her. The house was on her mother's property but Mae's uncle lived in it. The funny thing is that Mae didn't even need a deed to the house because it was all the same property which was situated next door to her mother, Big Momma's house. Big Momma had been a dutiful member of the Order of Eastern Star and had worked as a cook for the U.S. Army but

6

now she was very old and told stories of how as a newly freed slave, she ran all the time from the white men who chased her home from school. Cleo, her sisters and Granny and some of the older cousins said it wasn't true and that Big Momma got mixed up sometimes. Old or not, she owned all of the property, an acre of Indiana sub prime real estate and had final say on who got to stay or who had to go. There was even a cottage on the land for Tilly, Cleo's older sister and Marion's cousin Brandon, where they lived for a while.

With her own two hands, Granny laid some of the foundation for a screened porch. Granny's last boyfriend, Tommy, a mechanic, helped finance that project.

Marion was there with her friend Nicey, to watch the contractor Granny hired, pour cement for another addition to the house Uncle Jimbo still lived in. Although he promised after his death, a house he did not own to Mae, whilst he was alive, he was determined to hold on to it. He spent winters down south, completely turned off by the northern Indiana cold, so there was plenty of time for Mae to make the house livable.

The addition was a room for Mae's youngest daughter, Connie. Connie had wanted to move out but Granny convinced her to stay by promising an addition to the house where Connie would have the privacy she needed to complete her master's degree in library sciences. Connie felt it impossible to live in a world where she was always putting up with her many nieces and nephews going through the stuff in her room every time she was at school. The only change that happened after the addition was built was that it took a minute longer to get to her room and jiggle the lock open.

Mae insisted on wiring the addition herself instead of hiring an electrician but everything seemed to work fine. Kids don't notice much. It was too bad Tilly, the eldest of six sisters, had the home condemned and moved Granny to a senior citizen's building. Connie then got the single girl's apartment she so desired. Granny eventually accepted the move after a brief struggle. She had six daughters and she could not fight all six of them. Marion knew Granny was sad about the move. Her independence was important to her and she never, ever saw herself living around old people.

Marion spent a great deal of time with Granny growing up, as both of Marion's parents worked. Mae taught Marion all kinds of things, like how to gather old bricks from construction sites, dirt from construction sites, how to neatly pack your boyfriend's lunch (always making sure the corners of the wax paper surrounding the sandwich were creased and never crumpled). She also learned how to make a proper pot of black coffee and how to talk the manager of the lumber yard into a 20 percent off of a cord of 2 by 4s.

Marion heard earfuls about the struggle between Big Momma, Mae and Uncle Jimbo, sitting in the back of Granny's white Cadillac. Jimbo never wanted to give up his house but Mae was tired of renting the tar roof shack as she called it, and she had all those girls and was getting on in age and wanted a home of her own. Jimbo said after he died, Mae could have the property. By the time Mae got the house, most of her kids were married and had kids of their own. Connie was all she had left of her brood of women. The compromise is that Jimbo was getting on in years and it would be nice if Granny could look after her uncle a little more closely when he was up north. He slept on the porch Granny enclosed. The porch is what he liked best.

Gas Station Divas

Since they were now neighbors, Big Momma, from time to time would watch her great-grandchildren when Mae had extensive errand running to complete. Sometimes Mae took her older grandsons with her to run errands and left the younger Brandon and Marion behind. Jimbo and Big Momma liked to entertain the children with storytelling because they didn't believe in television and were born and raised on a farm down south. Storytelling is apparently one of the things sharecroppers did back then. Marion got the impression that migrating up north was an eventual reality that most farmers resisted as they promised to hold fast to the traditions of the Mississippi delta. During these storytelling sessions, Jimbo always told Marion and her cousin about his wife, who they had never met. He said how he was going to fix the house up for her. He was saving it, he said, in case his wife ever came back, which is why Granny couldn't have it yet. Every evening, Uncle Jimbo would set up camp on his porch, sip from a jar of homemade hooch until he was drunk, swat at flies and mosquitos and cry very loudly about his wife. Marion had never seen a man cry other than Uncle Jimbo. Jimbo himself was proper and always swaddled the jar in a brown paper bag when he drank from it. It was as if he had never left Mississippi or the farm. Eventually, Jimbo died of a broken heart and complications from alcoholism. Towards the end of his life, it was said that he accepted that his wife was not going to come back to him but they never got a divorce. Elvie eventually died right where she ran back to—her childhood home in Arkansas. She took care of her mother until she died. She was the perfect daughter but not that much of a good wife but Jimbo wasn't that good of a husband so they had at least that in common. Elvie whispered that she was ashamed to have her mother live in that shack Jimbo called a home, so she knew she had to plan because her mom was getting old and always asking when they were going to come get her. Elvie had a dad somewhere but Jimbo never cried about him and no gossip about him ever filtered down to the children.

Jimbo's wife wanted more out of life but she got married at 16 so she never quite made the connections she needed to social climb or have a nice house, Granny's daughters surmised. Elvie didn't understand alcoholism either, Granny said to Marion once, as she tossed shovels of rich black topsoil on top of an old sheet in the trunk of her white Cadillac. Marion asked her all the time why Uncle Jimbo cried, as she stood out of the way of Granny and her shovel.

By the time Marion was 12, it was clear why Elvie didn't stay. None of the home projects Jimbo planned ever panned out the way they should have and he fussed every time Granny made an improvement. The porch and plumbing were old and they still had an outhouse. Jimbo was always high, so it was probably difficult to think.

All Marion and her cousins knew is that they were not allowed to go near Jimbo's outhouse or Granny's cesspool and to never ask for anything to eat from Jimbo's house because he had roaches, it was said.

All of that changed once Granny moved in and made the improvements. Indoor plumbing and a yard without a cesspool were a step up. Granny finally had it all together and was proud of her creation. Her girls had always used any of Granny's homes as their base of operations but this one was different because there was so much more room and it belonged to her. The yard was beautiful. The barbeque cook-outs and kids running everywhere, hyped up on coolers full of pop drew nothing but pride from all of the women. Every time Mae's girls got together it was like an instantaneous party because there were so many of them.

Gas Station Divas

Too bad Mae had grown old working on the house and waiting for Jimbo to stop sleeping on the porch. He died on the porch in his drunken, tobacco chewing sleep. The house was finally all hers but the very people she set her mind to do for, ultimately did her in. Mae's daughters were worried about her obsession with fixing up the house. The very last straw was the DIY wiring project.

Granny had mentioned several times she wired her own home because she was proud of it but the only ones who seemed to care were the ones who spent the most time with her, which were the grandkids. It took Connie watching her mother make ongoing adjustments to the wiring and fiddling with the fuse box to really let sink in what was happening. The next thing Marion knew, Granny was in a two-bedroom apartment. She wanted two bedrooms in case her children or grandchildren needed a place to stay.

The children and had no parts of grown-up life except finding new ways to listen to their mothers' telephone gossip. Their days were spent as carefree children after school, not like kids of today enrolled in every discipline under the sun. Marion and Brandon and the rest of her cousins had to make up their fun or go in the house with Granny and watch Wild Wild West reruns, so skinned knees were ignored. Everyone had to keep up with the pack on his or her bike. Those days were gone and they were all grown with children of their own.

Marion's boring midwestern town was just that—boring like any other small town. Everyone knew one another so that meant kids had special rules: don't ask anyone for anything, don't go in anyone's house and don't ever tell what goes on in your own house because everyone gossiped. Marion thought nothing ever went on anywhere with anyone in her little hick town, so she didn't remember the lessons of her childhood because she did not find it useful. Much later and on down the road, those ignored lessons bit her in the ass.

###

CHAPTER 1
HELLO, SUNSHINE

Marion talks to herself frequently. And she's used to answering back. As she clip-clopped down the South Beach strip, her hair sort of just straggled along her shoulders, like straw. She had no job, no man, and no cares.

The only thing she had was money and a few sweat stains.

"I stink. And anyone looking can tell that my hair isn't really combed," she said, mumbling, juggling shopping bags and walking and sniffing her pits.

Marion pulled her shirt away from her body. She would learn to wear cotton in the South Florida sunshine--and no more thongs.

Some of her friends would claim her current situation was enough to care about. They all had relationships or husbands and Marion had nothing like that. She didn't seem to want anything like that and that is what troubled everyone. It was if she had given up.

Marion hefted her bags up the stairs to a waiting cafe table at Wet Willy's. One of their special frozen drinks and a perch to look at the men would complete her day. South Beach shopping and drinking made her forget all of her problems--which is the purpose of living in Florida instead of Indiana.

But it's really no place for little kids, she thought.

She ordered a strawberry margarita.

The waitress who bounced away to fetch the order, blond pony bobbling, seemed happy so Marion figured she had finally begun to make the right choices. Live in a happy place and be happy. The kids could adjust.

Besides, Miami Dade County and Broward County were very different. Regular people not celebrities settled into the relative quiet of Broward County. The local real estate agents had made it very clear that where she chose to buy a house was neither

Palm Beach County nor Miami Dade and wondered that if she had big money, why didn't she buy in Palm Beach County?

She understood their arguments but the baby mansion built into the rock of the shore line was what she wanted and buying that kind of home anywhere else would have left her broke. The company gave her enough money to go away on, not to live a lavish lifestyle like them. In other words, it was good enough for her. She accepted their offer of a few million without hesitation and left town.

Marion looked at the bags strewn about her. Shopping on the strip in South Beach gets respect--not everyone can do it. And there she was—a little country girl from Gary, Indiana who had done well enough to do it too. The difference is that it was after season and the beach was nearly empty. No true easterner would dare bare the hurricanes and the heat. It was the common folk and shop keeps who lived there. Tourists didn't count and celebrities are celebrities. They have many homes.

Marion relaxed a bit. It was humid and she tried to smooth her brown and blond-streaked, parted-down-the-middle-60s-layered-do with her open palms. She learned to forgo thick foundation. It served no purpose in a climate where pores have to be open for survival.

"This is like exercise. Kinda," she said to herself while dabbing at sweat rolling off of her forehead. It was as if someone had turned on a faucet. Her cold weather blood was still thick.

Summertime in Florida was for college kids and locals. Those of means had limos and Eastern Seaboard homes.

And were thin.

She looked down at the loop of flesh oozing around her midsection. Wrinkling her nose, she pulled on her poly blend shirt a bit. It wasn't a good look for her. She then pulled out her new leather large Coach Shopper from the box. She liked the classics. The smooth camel leather matched her new mules that, in the style of a rube, wore out of the store after buying them. But country is okay in Miami--it is still the south.

She took her time transferring the contents from her black Coach bucket into her new purse. The leather smelled good and mixed well with the sea mist in the air. The sun on the balcony of one of the most well-loved bars on the beach, gave little protection from the noonday sun.

"I love me," she said audibly and shaking around the contents of her new purse and fanning a little. Rumbling around in her new bag, Marion pulled out her phone. It was time to call mommy. She was about to hang up when her mom answered.

"Ma, what cha'll doin'?"

Nothing Marion, why. What do you want now?"

"Nothing just calling. How are the kids?"

"They're fine, when you coming to get them?

11

"Next week. Next two weeks. Can I talk to them? Gotta find another job and stuff.

"What kind of stuff? Girl what's wrong with you? Your daddy had the same job for 40 years—and then he retired," Mommy said.

She eagerly reached for the drink and handed the woman her credit card to open a tab.

"Ma, I'm a writer and things are different for me."

"So, you're going to start writing again?"

"Yes, what's wrong with that? I may even get into news again," Marion said.

"Can't you find some office job down there?"

Marion was silent.

"Didja get that money I sent?" she asked her mother.

"Yes, but you really ain't sending me any money cause most of it goes to feed and clothe your kids."

"I sent $1,400. I ain't broke. You need more?"

"No, but still... a woman down there by herself at your age. Why don't you come back up here and do something?"

"What ma, like get married—I just closed on a house!"

"Yeah? Sell it, come back up here and have some more kids or something. You could have bought a house up here," she heard her father say on the other line.

She sighed heavily because she didn't want to have this asinine conversation yet again.

"It would be nice but that's just not the path I'm on right now. It would be nice though. I'm gonna make some roots here in Florida so in about 20 years you and dad can have someplace nice to live."

"And watch your kids too, right?

"Yeah."

"Bye, Marion. Grow up. You are a 41-year-old divorced woman writing God knows what for whoever will pay you—what happened with that good job in Chicago you had? The news reports said they were having problems but..."

Mommy was droning on and on. Marion was quoted nearly every day on the debacle and Mommy hadn't noticed. Anyone can get tired of that. Marion didn't understand why her mother didn't understand. It didn't matter anyway because the whole company was looking to be somewhere else and Marion got out early.

"I told you. They were going out of business and they made me an offer. I have over $12 million in the bank," Marion said.

Her mother was silent on the phone. It was difficult to argue with money but she knew her daughter was not on the right path—mostly because she was out of her eyesight and didn't really know what she was doing.

Gas Station Divas

Marion felt frustrated talking to her mother. All of her aunts were overly involved in the lives of her children and her mom didn't understand why Marion, her eldest, purposely shut the door. She couldn't figure it and Marion didn't help much.

Every time Marion tried to share her plans and ideas with her mother, it was Mother who tuned-out daughter. So, Marion just stopped sharing her thoughts and ideas and went her own way.

"Ma?"

"Yeah, I'm here. You should be careful with your money. I didn't know you had that much saved up.""

"Oh, that is just part of it. My 401 K is separate."

"I guess being a spokeswoman paid well, sweetie but still, you need to be careful—and grow up."

"Bye. I'm gonna grow up. Don't worry," Marion said, taking another brain freezing slurp out of her drink.

"Are you drinking?"

"It's just a frozen drink ma."

"Bye Marion."

Marion could hear her children and her nieces and nephews in the background playing. She could also hear her mother immediately reporting to Dad.

"Marion ran her ass down to Florida with all that money and don't send shit up here—and she drinking!"

There was phone clattering and then a click. Mommy hung up.

The phone finally fell silent. She held her drink against her chest like it was the last bit of ice on the planet.

Florida was just supposed to be a vacation but she liked it there.

The children seemed sort of happy. One big happy family at least—the children seemed to love the break from mommy but she *was* on the deck of a bar drinking in the hot midday sunshine--not very motherly.

She knew she didn't want to stay in Indiana. She figured out long ago that she isn't her mother and could never be like her father mostly because those days were a part of an era gone by. Marion knew she had to make this work. Someone had to have need for a corporate writer, spokeswoman, or reporter—anything that paid well enough.

Hell, I can commercialize or spin anything. And still write a pretty decent news story, she thought to herself.

Continental Durable Medical Supply paid her pretty well when they were done with her--$12 million is enough to pad the way until the next job. She slurped on her drink. It was good--couldn't even taste the grain alcohol.

Gas Station Divas

Meanwhile, her friends could join her in a search for a new her. Momma could hold out a little longer with just a little bit more money. She pulled out her checkbook.

CHAPTER 2
THE MUDDRAKER

Marion text messaged Nicey. She figured that her husband *should* let her out of the house. Hell, he was never there anyway. One advantage to holding off on childbearing, she thought. Her phone rang in the middle of the message. It was Nicey.

"Hello?"

"Yeah, fool where you at now?"

"Miami"

"You moved to Florida?"

"Yeah, I'm sitting out here right now sippin' on a margarita. Y'all coming down here?

"Me and Toni--I don't know about Sheila. She got a job and a man."

"She ain't no fun no way. You bringing Tom?"

"If he wants to go. You know how you two fight."

"Shit, I ain't married to him—or Bobby. I don't have to do what any ol' man says for me to do," Marion said, wriggling her neck. She took another long suck of margarita. The waitress brought her another.

"Well if y'all come down here look me up."

"I'll be down there Wednesday but Toni said she can't come until the weekend."

"Okay. Where y'all staying?"

"We got a time share down there in Miami. Toni said she was bringing her new boyfriend so I don't know where she's staying. I haven't heard from her much. Shelia told me she changed her number again."

"Well she gotta keep the stray bitches off of her man—I don't blame her; however, I should be totally moved by the time you guys get here. I'm kinda short on furniture but we can have a cookout," Marion said.

"So, you have nowhere to sit but you have a barbeque grill. I hope this is the last time you have to move. You are acting so 'grish."

"'Grish?"

Marion thought about it for a while.

"Oooh, no you didn't just call me the N-word with ish on it!

"Yes, I did," her friend said, letting the phone go silent for a moment.

"You know Bobby likes you," Nicey said, changing the subject.

"Shit, I needed a job—or something."

"Yeah, you do—but not 1,500 miles away."

Marion was silent. She didn't want to get serious with Tom's friend Bobby.

"One of us stuck in Indiana is enough."

"Okay dear. We'll see you Wednesday."

"Alright."

She patted her hip pocket to make sure she had her keys. She called for the tab. It was hot, a very hot Saturday, and she was a little buzzed. Marion made it a habit of not telling all of her business. She didn't want her friends to know she didn't really have to work. She sat there for a minute. She didn't know why she extended the invite but now she had to go through with it.

She paid her tab, gathered her baggage and went on to search for where she parked her car. She had a lot to prove. Besides, she wasn't even sure if the fire pit actually qualified as a barbeque grill.

She took A-1-A home because she had no need to hurry.

The house was cool inside but messy. She kicked off her shoes and set her bags down.

She bought it because she really wanted to put down roots. All of the homes in the little community she chose came with an in-ground pool but she had an entire ocean as her backyard.

Deerfield Beach was a nice community. A-1-A ran along of what was considered her front yard, then the canal, then the homes within the gate. Somehow, they were all considered one community: Deerfield Estates.

Nature was her gate. She couldn't even see her property from the road. If it weren't for the 'For Sale' sign sitting out front against a small stone wall, she wouldn't have known a home was there.

She was glad for once that she locked her keys in the car or she would have never met Carl. He is the one who showed her how nice Deerfield Beach could be.

Carl Brandenstein came from wealth. He spotted her standing outside of his bank--cell phone in hand and a frown on her face. He cheered her up and then waited with her until AAA showed up with lock-out service. He was harmless and just curious about chocolate. He didn't want a whole plateful. He also didn't realize that there was a difference between African American females in Florida and those who come from up North—especially the ones who weren't born into wealth--like Marion.

She didn't have money in her pocket until seven years ago when she took the job as spokeswoman.

In spite of the differences, she showed him a good enough time, except after the wine n' dine, she did a dash. Still, he was nice, showed her around his home town and all. He helped her find a hotel near the ocean in which to stay and then he pretty much left her alone.

The kids would love Deerfield Beach because they've never had much more than an inflatable pool in the courtyard of their townhouse and had never lived in a warm climate. She knew they'd trip when no snow fell in December and they could grill Christmas dinner.

The grill disappeared at their old place. Now that is something the children were familiar with—theft, grime and general malaise. Grandma's house was only temporary but at least they had a backyard. And a bigger inflatable pool. And Grandma's grill.

But Marion had just purchased 9,200 square feet of South Florida sunshine.

The white piano in the corner, sunken living room with wall-to-wall white shag carpet and wet bar would keep her just fine. It was so futuristic and 60s at the same time. It was rather strange a brand-new master bedroom and bath and yet some of the home seemed untouched since being built.

The children each had their own room and there was a dining room, guest room, family room, a huge professional kitchen screened patio and huge vaulted ceilings in the living room.

Marion wondered why it came so cheap but she didn't care if someone died in the house. The bullet holes were patched up and there were plenty of pastors in town that would bless the house for a good tithing church member.

Everyone decent in Florida had a home in a gated community, a pool and a screened patio. She had a mansion built into the rocky shoreline.

"Maybe they won't notice I don't have any furniture, yet," she wondered aloud, surveying the room.

Besides some black barstools, and an Asian-inspired room divider, the house was empty but for love and a few pots and pans. She managed to move her three beds, three dressers, three televisions and an unimaginable number of toys from the townhouse. She felt bad that she had to sneak and move to Florida. Her parents didn't find out until they tried to use the spare key and found the locks changed.

She didn't have many DVDs and other electronics because she was never home enough to think to buy them. Her careers had kept her occupied and not thinking about home or a future without a specific career. She felt adrift. Besides, all of those electronics were for guys anyway. And she didn't have one. No man would have her, let alone live with her.

Either it was because her job kept her busy or because of his job but somehow it never seemed to work for long. She never wanted to live with any of them and at least twice it hurt the relationship.

She didn't know what to do so she escaped further into her career—which was more helpful than sitting around crying and wondering why her man wouldn't call her or take her out or spend quality time or open up or treat her with respect.

Her children were spoiled and her feet never stayed at home where a good woman's feet belonged—according to Mommy. Marion never fitted in well with the old-fashioned values that surrounded her. It didn't help she had been surrounded by some of the most powerful men in the area. Her life could have been seen as intimidating by the average man. Her boss and several of the board members had been so nice and supportive of her ideas. It seemed unreal.

She walked into the kitchen to get a glass of water. The house was filled with such sunlight and hope for the future. It didn't matter that she didn't have many material things filling it up. She left much of her favored lamps and other lights her mom gave her in an Indiana storage facility. Most of the time, she was drunk by the time she got home and that didn't matter either because there was no one there to see it. She didn't quite know what to do with her time, without the everyday grind of work.

But now newly rich, she had a new set of problems.

Taxes nibbled at her money. Most of it was in trust for the children, some tied up with the house, some in T-bills, Certificate of Deposits and a very conservative portfolio. Her money market would never be empty again--in spite of her shopping--but yet, she worried constantly of really going broke. She didn't have another backup plan immediately available.

She tried to curtail some of the shopping but it was so much fun and it felt so good. It was like mixing up sex and mind-altering drugs all together, except that she had something to wear later. It was like going blind and seeing nothing but a sweet, achingly erotic, orgasmic light that led you to where you next needed to be without thinking.

There were no decisions to make during the shopping trips because she could buy it all.

Marion, during her fits of shopping, didn't even bother to look for things for her home. She bought more clothes, some luggage and accessories. None of it reflected a need for putting down roots. And it's difficult to live in a Coach Leatherwear handbag.

Gas Station Divas

She hadn't bothered to check to see if the children were in a good school district or if there was a good after school care in the area. She was living in a wealthy area and wealthy people had nannies.

"I need a job," she heard herself say aloud standing in the middle of her house, surveying all that needed to be done. Her head was swimming.

It would be difficult to leave out being spokeswoman for a successful international medical supply company in any interview. She had been there only seven years but she was the face the public saw during the tough times.

Who could predict the financial corruption, the lawsuits, negligence and faulty equipment? Even she had been appalled by some of the claims. The media didn't even report half of the problems.

Matter of fact, she knew that during her time as reporter, she would have taken any spokeswoman to task for the outright lies she told. Her flashy demeanor deflected much of the attention away from the company. Locals seemed to be more interested in her and how she was living more so than how the company was being run.

Though the scandals—that fell one behind the other—were troubling, she handled it. She did whatever she thought she had to keep her job and most of the mud slung away from her and the company.

She walked into the kitchen and laid her face on the cool of the marble countertop. It had to be as old as she was. She held back tears. She was ashamed at how she felt. She knew she should be happy and that she didn't have to work but she wanted to because who would she be if she were not the Spokeswoman of a major corporation or a News Reporter?

"Hi, my name is Marion the News Reporter. Will you be my friend and show me how to be rich?"

Marion laughed at her silly thoughts and wiped tears away. She rubbed at her abdomen, and then she felt foolish. It was just her period making her cry.

Upon the purchase of her new home, Marion had felt empowered. Because of her previous work, she knew a few people. She attended a few benefits, got her photo taken with a few retired sports figures, attended luncheons but she couldn't make the jump, just yet. She didn't know how to become like them and not just fit in.

By their standards, she was rather broke and a bit of a threat. She was a single woman with some money, who wasn't gay, drug free and not necessarily on the prowl for a husband. She had more in common with the Spring Break kids than the society that she so desperately wanted to dazzle. But no one wanted to hear her stories at cocktail parties--the ones she could tell.

She had just enough money and name recognition to attend their events but not enough to get an invite to the house. Or go shopping with the limo service. To them, she was just a driver.

19

Gas Station Divas

All in the name of a job, she thought. Marion shook her head at herself and made her way to her bedroom. She couldn't nap. Thoughts ran through her head. The bad feelings were creeping in because she knew inherently, she did wrong. Marion wasn't raised to lie for herself or others but she did it.

Some of the deceptive schemes she came up with all by herself. In the end, the rewards were great but she wondered if she should have asked for more money. She never had a million of anything. She didn't know how long it would last. She had good references from work but with the scandal afoot, she couldn't figure how far it would get her. Who would trust their referrals?

She knew insiders would know about the legal proceedings, upcoming court dates. Maybe Mommy was right. Maybe she should have stayed close to home until this whole thing blew over and she really knew where she stood. The people at home still were kind to her and found other things to chit chat about. They knew she was only doing what she had to do but she was felt the growing distaste for her kind.

She flopped on the bed and turned on CNN. She was restless. She got up and peeled off her clothes and stepped into her steam shower. Her weave had begun to shed and she didn't have a regular beautician yet.

When she got out of the shower, some of the company execs were being shown on B-roll footage, again. She remembered when they shot that. It was the day she left town. She left the press conference and kept driving. She had already arranged for the kids to stay with her parents, her stuff was in storage and her bags were packed.

She had nothing but some maps, diet soda and some candy. It was the longest she had gone without drinking alcohol. She didn't even know how long it would take her to get to Florida but she knew she had to go and she did--with tears in her eyes. She felt like a fugitive of sorts. She even changed her cell phone number.

She slipped into her bra and sundress and rolled unto the bed again. She sifted through the covers to find her laptop. Most days not spent shopping or bar hopping were spent inside in the bed. She surfed the job sites, e-mailed her friends racy links and participated in several discussion board sites—and she had her photos.

There were exactly 1,237 photos of her favorite male hunk movie stars on her hard drive. She, for years, had been secretly obsessing over them--not like a normal fan but if she were a photographer she would get arrested for stalking.

Her friends refused to discuss the photos anymore. Nicey threatened to call a psychiatrist and report her. Toni just figured she needed a boyfriend. Bobby didn't know. He was always available to her but she shied away. It felt too good to be with him, so it wasn't easy to push him away. Instead, she spent hours going through and trying to acquire more photos.

The photos had been a distraction for some time. Once, when things started to get bad at work, she blew off a press conference just to spend time in bed going

20

Gas Station Divas

through them. She told the company vice-president she was sick and that didn't go over well at all. If it had not been for her giving up her season passes to the Bulls games, Neal would have been really sore at her. He was the lowest on the totem pole in terms of executives and he didn't handle the press well but when she wasn't there, he had to stand in for her.

Now, she was spending the time that she could have been using to prepare for the arrival of her guests in bed with some j-pegs.

She wanted a man—a perfect man--to come into her life and the photos were the closest she could get. Whenever she wanted a man, she would gaze at her photos for hours --she controlled it.

It was the impetus for moving to Florida—control of her own life.

She lay back on the soft pillows. She thought about getting a vibrator to save her manicure then she laughed. She would never let a man tangle his fingers in her hair because some of her wefts would surely land on the floor.

A knock at the door woke her out of her nasty little daydream.

It was the UPS man again.

"Package for Mr. Donovan." He pushed the electronic signing board towards her. She put her hands on her hips.

"He doesn't live here anymore. I bought the house. Why do you guys keep trying to deliver his packages here?" Marion said.

The cute UPS driver smiled, hunched his shoulders and walked away.

"This is like every week you guys are here, leaving these little yellow slips of paper on my door," she said.

He kept walking.

Unlike her former co-workers, Marion didn't have much to do. She returned to her bed and her photos.

She did whatever she could to push away the bad feelings. She tried to sign up for Peapod so that she could get out of grocery shopping but somehow that didn't exist in her area yet.

Marion was hungry and all she had in her refrigerator was half a bottle of Cîroc Vodka, some butter and some turkey bacon. So, she dug around in her purse for some Skittles she ran across during the purse transfer and chomped on them.

CHAPTER 3
DURABLE MEDICAL
SUPPLY

"Mothafuck that bitch. She ran her ass out of here with the money in her hand. She basically said fuck me and fuck you too. Why take up for her?"

"I don't know, Key. I don't know. I heard you should keep your enemies closer. You don't know where she is." Chuck said.

"Besides, what can we do? I'm calling lawyers right now."

Keith slammed the phone down. He had well known anger control issues and his head was hurting.

Chuck Eriks and Keith Vallejo worked with Marion on many of the anti-smear campaigns. Theirs was one of the few companies that still had in-house public relations teams. However, neither man got a deal. They were still stuck there at the company under federal investigation for corporate fraud. Keith hated to admit Chuck was right. He didn't know where Marion was—didn't know much about her but they knew a lot about the company. Both men needed her testimony.

They were told not to worry about it, get a lawyer and keep working. It didn't seem right to Keith but as long as he was getting a paycheck, he had no choice but to show up to work. He couldn't see anyone hiring him and he had no one to turn to.

His lawyer was about to be his best friend.

He knew he had to find Marion. She was gone and he was stuck and he didn't know what to do. She *could* be a good character witness or something. They had never really had a falling out. His side business had come to a screeching halt. He figured if he were to get prison time, it would be over transporting illegal substances and guns in their equipment shipments. No one seemed to pay much attention to what was going on and everyone was making money. He figured Marion's bright and shiny reputation could be helpful if he got the endorsement.

He had a cousin in the islands with all types of connections and always told him if he wanted to join the business to let him know so that's what he did. It was easy too.

Dock workers loaded the same boxes they had been—no weight change. It was easy to hide a few gun parts inside some of the surgical equipment because it was huge and they weren't greedy. Heroin, raw coca and gun parts. He started a day labor business and supplied all of the workers courtesy of his cousin, who packed what they needed inside the equipment after it was on the ship. No one checked, no one asked.

When it arrived at the U.S. port, it was checked but no one ever found anything hidden inside the CT scanner parts, respiratory machines or the barrels of special powder used to make casts. When the truck picked it up from the port, the men on the loading dock knew what went where. Everyone was happy. Besides, shipments were erratic and he knew when there would be a special delivery.

When Marion came on board with Continental Durable Medical Equipment, he was glad that she was cute. When he found out she would be his boss, he was still glad she was cute because he planned to fuck her. He had been at the company two years and managed to coast on charm and the good ol' boy network.

He didn't figure her to be scandalous because she was cute. Before he knew it, she was out front. But it's not that he ever wanted to do the same because falsifying financial reports and lying to investors was enough for him--but he thought those acts deserved a big payday too and more so than Marion. He felt betrayed but at least she wasn't meddlesome.

He heard Marion slept her way to a big payday and knew about the claims and the feds. They worked together only-- he never asked her out. They, along with most in the department, shared a late dinner at work a few times but never had sex. She didn't seem interested. Besides the only way he could sleep his way to a big payday was to be open to all players.

Most of the women were old or fat or both and the only gay man he knew of worked in the mail room. He wouldn't get much mileage out of that. He realized then that he was never a player in the game--should have gotten out--but he couldn't just change jobs.

Now, he needed a lawyer and it just hurt to know Marion maybe could have given him a heads up on what was going down. He felt abandoned—like he did as a teen when his parents abruptly told him adios a month after his high school graduation.

He didn't know what he would do then and he didn't know what to do now. The company wouldn't pay for a lawyer because they acted like they didn't want him there anyway so he was planning on keeping a low profile.

23

Chuck didn't have it any better. He was in the same boat so maybe they could go in on an attorney. Their IRA could be a source of money but if what was happening to investors spread to employees, that money would be gone too.

Keith picked up the phone to call employee relations. He knew they pretty much emptied out of the building before five.

***

Co-workers at the All-American Quick Stop teased Francis about she and Ron becoming a couple. They referred to him as her boyfriend behind his back and giggled when he was around. He was in there every day and not only because he got free coffee and soda but because the girl knew a lot about the streets. He was impressed. He would tell her who in her neighborhood just got arrested and she would ask why police activity was spotted here or there.

Usually he knew of police arrests but it wasn't because he was involved. As a Florida State Trooper, he was involved with task force activities upon request. Most of what he told her was gossip and hearsay. She was a nice rest stop and shelter from the hot sun. Being a motorcycle cop was tough but he looked good doing it. He hated having to be on traffic duty but his rookie years were long gone. It was an easy shift and he didn't have to be tied to a desk all day. He was free.

Today wouldn't be any different. He promised himself he would stop hanging around her—he didn't want to be involved and she had some shady friends and it could get messy.

"Hey, girl," he said, flashing a smile. She had her naughty Catholic schoolgirl look today. Heavy eye makeup, teased hair, white button-down shirt --unbuttoned and that dark lipstick she was so fond of.

Francine's face lit up when Ron walked in. She only had 20 minutes left on her shift but staying over could put extra pay on her check and she needed to inventory the cigarettes anyway.

"Let me get these customers out of the way," she said.

Ron poured himself a huge cup of Diet Coke.

It was helpful for police to feel welcome at the All-American Quickie Mart to stave off robberies. It didn't hurt when they were cute and flirted a lot.

Francine's manager was watching them on the closed-circuit camera and gossiping with her husband.

"Harold you ought to see this heffa. She is grinning from ear-to-ear 'cause that cop rolled up in here," Helen Tompkins said.

"Maybe you ought to be smiling up in my face when you get here. I think she has the right idea," her husband said.

"You are so nasty. We've been married a thousand years and you still want to do it every day," she giggled.

"Well, are you on your way home?""

Gas Station Divas

"Yeah, Frannie will stay anyway because Ron is here. She gets a little overtime and I get to come home. At least I can trust her," she said.

Helen still turned her husband on and it thrilled her. Everything she did, she did to impress him: the tight slacks, the crazy diets, nails, hair—all of it. She finally got a husband and she intended on keeping him. It was good that she finally shed the image of the damaged goods woman—single, unmarried, three kids, and three different sperm donors. She finally got her tubes tied and a job at the gas station. She gave up on finding a husband. Then she met Harold.

On purpose or not, most of the women she hired had been teen moms. She felt for them. Some you couldn't keep on because they stole or lied too much or were just lazy. Frannie was almost like a daughter to her. Every time she extended responsibility to her she accepted it with glee. She was hungry to climb a ladder of success—even one as assistant shift manager at the neighborhood gas station.

She was also good to keep certain customers coming back. The low-cut tops and funky stripper style shoes made her a bit of a celeb—even though halfway through her shift she had on her black tennis shoes. She always had something on her body to look at or in Ron's, case touch.

"Frannie, I'm outta here,'" Helen yelled from the back of the store.

"You gone boss?"

"Yeah. Stacy should be here soon to relieve you but could you stay a little bit over to keep an eye on her?"

Francine looked at Helen with that look. A smile crept across her face. It was a game they played. They both knew she wanted to work over anyway.

"Yeah, I have to count the cigarettes anyway," she said.

Helen smiled and with a wave left Ron and Francine alone in the store. She couldn't explain it but lately when Ron was around she would get nervous and her stomach would churn. It felt good.

Customers came in waves, mostly showing up all at once. The store was easier to get to than the grocery store and they sold beer and wine. It was nice having Ron on hand when the drunks came in or the speed freaks looking for those damn pills. She hated dealing with the "all-natural uppers" because she had to complete a Drug Enforcement Agency log for each purchase and they always had decoys coming in to trip her up.

It was easy to go to jail working at the All-American Quickie Mart.

Francine pulled out the cigarette racks above the register got out her clipboard and started counting cigarettes.

Ron watched her as she reached up to the very top of the cigarette racks perched on a step stool.

Her ass was huge. Ron wondered why she didn't become a stripper like most of the girls in her project—the ones who could do it at least. At least she wasn't turning

25

tricks. Although Francine worked every day, living in Palm Beach County was expensive but it was all she knew. She requested upon hire to not work in any of the West Palm Beach All-American Quickie Marts because she didn't want her whole block asking for free stuff or trying to steal stuff just because she was there.

"What you getting into tonight, Frannie?" Ron said, breaking the awkward silence.

"I don't know. It depends on if my mother will babysit and if she has any plans. Why? You offering?" Francine stopped counting and looked at Ron seductively.

"Naw, I'm wondering, miss. I read in the paper your boy got some federal time on that case."

"What boy?"

"Dude that was pulled over with all that 'cain in his car. He didn't have tags or insurance and he was drunk," Ron said, sucking his teeth.

"Dumbass."

Francine heard herself sigh audibly. She put the clipboard down. and pretended she didn't know.

"Forreal? I didn't get to read the paper today."

Francine happened to be sitting on the porch when the entire ruckus started. One of her girlfriends called her crying from the scene talking about can she help with bail or did she know a lawyer.

Francine was tired of knowing people like that. She was mad that Ron knew she talked to people like that and that she lived in the 'hood.

"All right then. You working tomorrow?

"Yeah, I'll be here in the morning. You leaving already? Stacy isn't here yet."

"Yeah, I got a date tonight."

It was as if a heat bomb went off inside her body. Her face was hot and her ears were ringing. His words slapped some reality into her but she held her stance and smiled.

"Oooh, look at you! Be safe out there Ron," she said, a little too quickly. Francine stepped down from the little stool she was standing on and smiled a little more, smoothing down her smock and folding her hands across her huge chest.

"You know it, girl. I guess you're straight days now, huh big time?"

Ron laughed a little on his way out of the store. He swung his powerful leg over his cycle and pulled off with a roar. He hoped that would set things straight between them. It was also a reason to keep befriending those types of women. They were street and they played it cool. He was glad it was starting to drizzle a bit. He felt bad and the rain distracted him. He knew better than to bring a woman like that into his life.

Francine watched him whiz away on his motorcycle. She had to hold on to the counter to keep from falling. She felt weak, physically. She couldn't believe it. She

26

was only 29. She thought to herself that she was too old to run after men anymore but she was too young to be an old maid.

Although they had not officially had sex she had fooled around with him enough to be hurt.

Through her fog, she saw Stacy walking toward one of the entrances. She was early for once. And looked really fat.

She called Sherry and put on her headset so she wouldn't have to interact with Stacy.

"Hello?"

"Sherry, why did that fool just tell me he got a date tonight?"

"Girl naw, Ron? He played you? He didn't seem like the type and he a cop!"

"Well, hoe cop—that's what he is."

There was silence between the women. Once again, the hurt and the pain make another bitter conversation.

"Sherry, you still there?" Yeah, but I don't understand why you are upset. You guys weren't really going together. He never asked you out."

"We fooled around a little and he didn't have to take me out to make me like him."

"Did you tell him you liked him?" Sherry asked.

"No, but I won't get the chance now. He has a date tonight. He's dating," Francine said.

"Well, you should date too, girl. Don't let him get you down. I mean, it will pass. Y'all not fighting, are you?"

"No, we wouldn't have anything to fight over—except this!" Francine said.

Sherry could hear her talk to customers and make change.

"You still at work?"

"Yep. You got some beer?"

"Yep—but bring some more. We'll need it tonight 'cause I know you fixin' to trip," Sherry said.

Francine's face felt as if it was made of stone she was so mad. She was glad to have Sherry's friendship and understanding and that she could take her kids with her and not ask anyone to babysit for her.

"Ask your boy to roll one for ya friend," Francine said.

"Damn, you must be pissed. All right. See ya when you get here."

Francine clicked off her phone and handed down instructions to Stacy on how to inventory the cigarettes. She took off her smock and folded it up. She couldn't help but stare at Stacy's bulging stomach area. Stacy turned away. Frannie grabbed two six packs of Mickey's Big Mouth Malt liquor and slapped the money on the counter.

"Be careful on that step stool, girl," she warned with a frown.

27

CHAPTER 4
NICEY & TOM ARE SWEETHEARTS

Nicey and Tom were the most popular couple in their city. They went to all of the right balls and galas, donated to the right charities, had the picture-perfect life-- and above all they still loved one another and got along. But they rarely spent more than 30 days straight, together. Alone.

Marion and Nicey were the best of friends and they had been friends since the seventh grade. Marion and Nicey shared their friends, so parties the women threw were enormous.

This trip to Florida would be more like a mini spring break than a second honeymoon. Niecy and Tom liked to have fun together. And bringing

Bobby would make it a foursome--all that much more fun. Marion didn't necessarily need to know that Toni and Shelia refused the invite to yet another one of Marion and Nicey's escapades. Besides they were pretty settled into their relationships and didn't want to rock the boat. Nicey thought maybe she should have married an old-fashioned man. It's not like she didn't try but secretly, she felt good about her life—she just pretended to have regrets.

She was looking forward to the trip because they might even meet some more swingers while they were there. Tom got Nicey into swinging exactly 45 weeks after they were married. It's almost as if it was planned that way.

Of course, there was resistance at first but after meeting Bobby and his wife Tamara then Lester and Carri she knew she would never go back to regular married life. She got used to watching her husband glare at the breasts of other women. And a good thing for Tom because he knew he couldn't love anyone else. At least he picked for her, attractive, endowed men who were nice to her before plowing into her.

He had nerves of steel to introduce her into his lifestyle. But to look at Tom, one would ever know and he liked it that way. Niece sat up in the bed and gently shook Tom.

"Is Bobby still going?"

Anymore, they didn't have much sex without the swinging. Tom was sound asleep.

"Tommy!"

"What. Yeah, he's going. He ain't got nothing better to do."

Bobby's wife Tamara left him after a particularly interesting coupling with a West Indian couple last year. Hadn't seen or heard from Tamara or Rufus, since. He didn't know their marriage was in that much trouble. Marion had been helping him soothe some of the pain with their long talks but now she was gone too.

Bobby dared not tell Marion about the swinging. Besides it was married couples only. She didn't need to know just yet. Bobby looked to only float through life now, numb and only surviving each day.

Chapter 5 Agent of Love 007 Ron Bowling

Continental Durable Medical Supply International stayed in the news. There was always a new development. She could no longer look backward. She bought a used treadmill from eBay and started walking 20 minutes a day.

When she finally got around to the store, she decided to go all out at Whole Foods. She bought a pound of caviar and some smoked salmon just to impress her friends. Besides, she still wasn't sure what to do with the firepit.

A trip to the liquor store found her at the Johnnie Walker isle. She bought Blue Label. Cheapness is a habit hard to break but she was breaking it.

The heat in Florida took some getting used to. Whenever Marion left the cool of a store, the heat radiating from the pavement would singe her nostrils. Most of people of means left after season to return to their Hampton estates and such--Marion would come to understand.

Combined with the new exercise routine, she felt like hell warmed over—which calls for a mandatory dip in the ocean. It was her new best friend. She then slept the day away after a shot or four of Johnnie.

Marion awoke to the realization that her friends would soon be in town and she still was not prepared. She jumped out of bed as if she were late for work.

The hot shower felt good. The powerful shower jets surrounded her in the luxurious marble master bath. It was one of the selling points for the house. And the fact that the whole house was set into stone that lined the shore of the ocean was even better.

People who lived in Deerfield Beach who had money, snubbed the runt mansions lining the coastline, choosing the newly built homes further inland.

She turned the steam nozzle up a little in the shower to clean her pores. She wanted her skin to glow in case Bobby came with Tom and Nicey.

She perked up in the shower and begun to think about the day ahead. Being an early riser was helpful with all the goofing off she had done.

She had to shop for more food and needed to buy bed linen for three beds.

Marion stepped out of the cool of her home into what was real—the hot Florida sunshine and 100 percent humidity.

It was enough to make her cuss. She flopped down into the car seat—which was leather and hot--and jumped back out. She reached back in to start the Cobalt Blue M6 Convertible BMW—definitely not a mommy car.

The remote starter dangled from her key chain and she looked at it. She stood in the driveway for a while, rubbing the back of her leg and looking at her watch and her car. She went inside the house grabbed her shopping list, locked the door behind her and got inside the car.

"Damn!" Come on air, work." She pulled away and noticed that she needed gas. She headed to a nearby gas station.

The store was shockingly cool and the line was long. She walked the isles and grabbed a water and then a cup of coffee. She looked around self-consciously.

"No time for Starbucks today," she said with a smile to a State Trooper who was also getting coffee. She really wasn't one for gas station coffee.

"You ought to put some ice in it. It's hot out today," he said, smiling back. He grabbed a large cup and filled it with ice and handed it to her.

Marion accepted the cup and the flirt.

"It's hot everyday around here, isn't it?"

"Yes, ma'am it is." Tall, dark and handsome smiled at her, tipped his hat and jumped back onto his motorcycle.

"Damn, you look good in those boots," she thought to herself.

She poured the sugary coffee into the cup and dumped vanilla bean powder and half and half over it, shaking it as she headed to the counter.

"Do you have a Speedy Gas Card?" the chirpy girl behind the counter said.

"No, what's that?"

The girl handed Marion an application. She filled it out and handed it back.

The girl swiped the card.

"You saved 20 cents per gallon on your gas today," she said, handing her back the card.

Marion thanked her and clomped outside to pump her gas.

The state trooper was still there, admiring Marion's butt.

"You aren't from around here are you?"

"Nope, how could you tell."

"You don't have an accent. Mostly everyone down here is from Europe or an island."

"You don't have an accent either. Where are you from?"

"Indiana."

"No, really—I am too!"

Francis looked out from behind her register at the cute cop flirting with someone other than herself.

"See what giving it away free get you?" She said to her co-worker, pointing.

31

Gas Station Divas

"Ooh girl, he wrong for that. What you going to do?"

"You mean what will I do, that won't result in me getting a ticket or going to jail?"

"Yeah, you right about that."

Both ladies turned to the customers waiting in line.

You know what Sherry? I won't do anything. I will let each woman find out on their own—that way they'll go through what I did. Nobody told me anything."

"That's wrong too, girl." Sherry said.

State Trooper Ron Bowling handed Marion his card before hopping on to his motorcycle with a roar. He didn't get far before pulling over a motorist--mostly to show off. He could see Marion standing beside her car watching him.

CHAPTER 6
BOBBY AND MARION
AREN'T SWEETHEARTS

Sherry didn't live in the Fareview Housing Development like Francine. She lived in a nice, cool area of West Palm Beach where neighbors were neighborly but only to a point. Mrs. Kravitz would have gotten her feelings hurt in their world. Sherry lived with the dope man in their four-bedroom home, which was nicely appointed.

They had cookouts and the resemblance of normalcy. Ross was never home and no one asked questions, especially Sherry.

"I just went in his stash and rolled one. He won't mind," Sherry said, holding up the joint after opening the door for her friend. She was the one who got Francine the job. Francine frequented the gas station from time to time on the way to the clubs and Sherry had seen her around. The women struck up a running friendliness. It helped also that they had friends in common. Most of Sherry's relatives lived inside of Fareview.

"I can tell—you can't roll, Francine said.

"Whatever, loser," Sherry said.

Francine playfully kneed her friend in the butt as they retired to the kitchen. Francine re-rolled the joint. Although she had not smoked marijuana in years-- for several different reasons--she felt she needed a puff or two. No one checked for drug use at the gas station. She opened up a Mickey's Big Mouth and relished the cool, pale liquid as it bit its way down her throat.

"I haven't had a Mickey's in a while," Sherry said, looking through the green barrel shaped bottle. She secretly longed to open a bottle of wine but decided to suck it up for a friend. She didn't think Frannie could appreciate an aged bottle of wine.

She looked at her friend and felt sad for her. Frannie passed her the joint. Sherry sharply pulled the smoke out of the rolled cigarette and into her lungs. She handed it back and turned Tyra Banks on the little TV in the kitchen. The subject was infidelity and Francine lowered her head to the counter, and shielded her ears.

***

Marion was nicknamed the "Golden Diva" by Francine and the girls behind the counter. She had a look of self-satisfaction on her face as she entered into the store to get change back from the pump. Her cheapness was a habit. She had gotten into the habit over the years, of putting only a few dollars into the tank at a time. In the hot South Florida weather, AC is a must. Gas tanks need to be filled. All of the women there had seen the display between Ron and Marion and it wasn't appreciated as they were a rather tightly knit bunch. The sun had burnished Marion's skin into a bronze glow, almost matching her hair. She glimmered.

The rude girl behind the counter almost threw the money at her.

"Potbellied bitch..." Marion grumbled under her breath.

The woman watched Marion try to switch in those ridiculously high heels as she stomped back to her car. She didn't know what the problem was but she didn't appreciate rudeness.

"That big-booty hoe gone git hers. Wait until she comes back in here," the clerk said, neck wriggling.

Marion slid into the comfort of her Beemer--it was proving its worth in attracting BMW (Black Men Working) and she liked that.

"Forget them gas station divas in there. I got my shit together," Marion said, punching the gas pedal with a flick of her gold-streaked hair.

It was off for a spa facial, pedicure and manicure—a world those girls would never experience, and she knew that. Right then, at that thought, she felt bad.

When she returned home, the guard at the gate handed Marion a note upon her arrival.

We were here but where are you? Call-612-412-4567.

She thanked him and u-turned her car around. It was Nicey. She called the cell phone number.

By the time Marion arrived at the South Beach condo Niece and Tom owned, the impromptu party was underway—pool, Bobby and all.

"We brought someone for you!" Nicey said.

"Ummhn, he right out there," Tom said, never turning away from the golf tournament. Marion looked at her friend and then at the back of Tom's head. She

Gas Station Divas

wanted to flip that couch over with him on it. He must have felt it because he turned around and looked at his wife and his wife's friend.

They were all waiting on her response.

"Okay. I didn't bring a suit." She lowered her head nearly to her chin and turned away.

"You know Marion, you just up and ran off. Those people paid you and you split. The only way I knew where you were is because I ran into your mother at the mall. You left Bobby behind without a second thought. You can at least be nice," Niece said.

"I was just taking the advice I was given. The owners said I should use the money to explore other options in other states—if you get my drift. I wasn't dating Bobby—I-I-I wasn't even thinking about him. I was in survival mode. Where is Sheila and Toni?" Marion said, distracted and uncomfortable.

Niece hunched her shoulders and Marion put her face in her hands. She had been on such a great sunny Florida day high and then this great crash of reality was too much. She sat her purse down and walked out to the pool area.

"Hey boy. What you doin', Marion said in an almost fake-chirpy voice. She was nervous.

Bobby splashed around in the hot tub and said, "Damn."

"You look good. Where ya' been?" he continued.

"Here. Buying a house and stuff......" Marion said. She rambled about this and that, Bobby looking at her with his bright brown eyes, soaking her in and holding her there.

The pauses and silences were difficult.

"You've been through a lot lately. How are you holding up?" Bobby said.

Marion's eyes welled up. It had been difficult and she had been scared. She was down there in Florida by herself and it would be nice to have a familiar shoulder to snuggle into.

"It's been alright," she said looking at the floor and wiping the mist out of her eyes.

Bobby stood up and Marion's eyes followed. He looked so good and she was so weak and needed a hug.

"I missed you when I found out you were gone. I know we weren't really kicking it anymore but the idea that I could call you and maybe come over and we get together was nice—I dunno—comforting or something. I was kinda hurt when I found out you were gone. Matter of fact, I was kinda upset," Bobby said.

He couldn't believe he said it either. Those were just thoughts rolling around in his head, soliloquies he recited to himself when he was pissed and pacing around his house. He didn't realize that he was actually saying anything until he looked at her

35

face. She looked like a hurt, lost angel—crooked halo and all. She was sitting there, hair straggly as usual and looking as if she was all his to have all to himself forever.

But she wasn't and he knew it but he kissed her anyway.

Inside, Niece was pretending not to look out the window.

"Oh my God! He just cupped her little face in his hands and kissed her. Oh my God! They're in love Tom. Lookit," Niece said, pointing. Tom stretched his neck around to look.

"I knew it. That's why she ran. She don't do nothing else nobody tells her to do but she gone come all the way down here by herself talking about the company told her to do it. That's why I told Bobby to come. I knew they were in love," Tom said.

Niece just looked at him. Tom had the nerve to claim credit. He didn't even want to come down there. She had to get him drunk on the flight down to keep his ass focused on something else besides complaining.

"Yeah, baby I know," she said, with a sigh. Soon, they were kissing too.

The pair came inside for a bit.

"Girl, let's make a liquor run," Marion said. Nicey jumped up off of the couch, grabbed purses and tumbled out of the door.

"Oooh girl, I feel soooo good! I don't know what happened," Marion said.

"I'm so glad Bobby came down. I knew it," her friend said.

They were best friends. They had shared everything since the seventh grade.

"Why don't we move the party to your house? Is it set up? Are you all moved in?" Nicey said.

Marion paused. She opened her mouth and nothing came out.

"What. Do you have furniture?" she said.

"Well kind of I do---I have a bed—a king sized Tempur-Pedic bed and some patio furniture.

"Oooh you so nasty! Slut! Talking about all you have is a bed!"

"Let's swing by and pick up the house a bit. I want Bobby to not be too shocked," Marion said.

Niece shook her head in agreement. When the women arrived at Marion's home Nicey's mouth fell open.

"Oh my God! Is this you? How much did those people pay you? Oh my God Marion, what have you done?"

"Enough to get this. Isn't it fabulous? I love it too. It's what I always imagined myself having," Marion said.

"Are you running from the law?" Niece said.

"Naw, but they chasing me!" Marion said. The women jumped around in excitement.

"Girl, I would have moved too. Look at how well you've done. You have the car you've always wanted—an M6 convertible BMW..." Niece's voice trailed in and out

36

while walking around the house. Her eyes welled up. She was speechless. She walked to the living room to get a better view of the ocean.

"Come on let's sit out on the patio. The former owners left their patio furniture behind. It's actually quite nice," Marion said.

The women sat together in comfortable silence, each feeling the soft ocean breeze against their bodies. It was relaxing.

Niece broke the silence mid-thought. She had been rolling the night around in her mind.

"Girl, I saw you and Bobby together and it was so sweet."

"I couldn't help it. Six foot four, tan, good hair--good everything. He can be sweet as pie sometimes. I was so glad to see him that I got carried away."

"Tommy hasn't been intimate with me in a while. I guess I'm just tense. This is supposed to be a second honeymoon-quickie thing so maybe it will get better tomorrow, Nicey said.

"And still we have the whole weekend," Marion said.

"You right. Hey go crack open that Johnnie Walker I saw behind the bar.

There's liquor here?

"Yeah, didn't you know?

"Naw, girl. I've barely been here since I bought the place,"

Marion went inside to the wet bar and saw that there were quite a few bottles available and a note:

"Please enjoy this as my uncle would have. He loved life."

Marion set the note aside. She planned to save it. She poured herself and Niece two fingers of the fine Blue Label scotch. She ran to the kitchen for lemons and soda and a silver serving tray.

While the women sipped and talked, Tom called to get find out what happened to the liquor run.

"The drinks are here at Marion's," she told her husband.

She gave him directions and hung up. The women waited in comfortable silence. What Niecy told her rolled around in her head—that she and Bobby were in love. It couldn't be farther from the truth. Niecy figured that Marion would never figure men out. She thought they had the perfect marriage.

Tom and Niece didn't stay long after touring the house. Marion and Bobby snuggled on the patio then headed in for a lover's shower. They had only been together one other time. The kisses were passionate and deep. He slid himself into her mouth--he was so huge. Marion gazed up into his eyes. She could see love but what she was feeling was lust. Same old problems. She thought about this as she ran her tongue around the tip of his manhood and down the length before plunging it deep into her throat. She could taste him but he pulled out and slid deep inside her moist thighs.

They made love like they were making a baby. It was good. Too bad all Bobby wanted to really do is cut her wings. Marion knew it wouldn't last so she just enjoyed it. When they got to the bed, she rolled him over onto his back and rode him like they would never meet again.

CHAPTER 7
RON & MARION

The next morning was filled with questions.

"What did last night mean?" Marion said.

"What do you want it to mean?" Bobby said.

"Sex," Marion said, leaning over to kiss him.

"If that's what you want it to be then that's what it is, okay?"

Marion nodded in agreement.

"Want some breakfast?" she asked coquettishly.

The pair spent the morning together like lovers on vacation.

Bobby was impressed with the house and the car--impressed that Marion had enough sense to spend her money on either.

Usually, she spent her money on clothes and shoes and purses. Cramped into that little townhouse with her kids—he used to lecture her on money management and homeownership.

He was a pretty sensible guy and had done well for himself in the public service sector as a civil engineer.

He invested and saved well so he lived well. He always lectured Marion on how she spent her money because she hadn't bought a house in Indiana or a really nice car. He didn't understand that her job was all encompassing and she hadn't focused much on creature comforts. Her last few years were spent putting out fires.

People recognized her most of the time and then things would get out of hand sometimes. The public saw her as the face of one of the largest employers in the area and an insider who could be responsible for the internal strife within the company. People pulled at her constantly so she made it a habit to keep a low profile which included staying indoors a lot or conducting personal business out-of-area, in peace. Marion stockpiled her money in the bank like old folks. She hadn't diversified anything and did good to put it all in a money market. That had been the extent of her financial savvy.

Now, it was different. The money market was still her greatest idea yet and although she was quite comfortable with the runt mansion in Broward and the expensive convertible, it was arguable if a convertible was the appropriate mommy car for her and her two children. It was arguable if beachfront property was kid friendly. She was beginning to grow up a bit and question her motives. She didn't want to be a selfish little girl anymore.

"Do you think about how your children will react to having to move down here?" Bobby asked while they were walking to the bistro to get breakfast.

"Yes, I did. They're going to be happy wherever I decide to live because we will be together. We're all going to be happy here in Florida. My parents or you for that matter may not like it but we will," Marion said.

Bobby took the rest of the ride in silence. It stung that she on purpose pointed out that she was looking out for herself and kids and not him. He knew he shouldn't have asked her a future question--he didn't even see a future with them together but he asked. He felt like a bitch riding in the passenger seat of her life. He was going to take the wheel on the way back.

Tom and Niece were already at the beachfront Italian breakfast nook she had told them about last night. Marion had discovered the place as she walked around her neighborhood last week. She felt so privileged to have such a nice thing to present to her friends.

Bobby was silent for most of the black coffee and hard roll breakfast he had ordered. He lectured Marion on the benefits of eating light as she plowed into a cheesy concoction with rich Italian espresso, sugared up to country-assed perfection and lightly shaken together with iced half and half.

"You talking about eating healthy, at least you can have a glass of orange juice with that jail meal you ordered. Coffee and a hard roll--what's wrong with you?" she said playfully.

Bobby didn't smile as much as he snorted out a response.

"You gone get fat," he said.

It seemed as if the tinkle of glass and fork came to a quiet stop. Everyone on the patio seemed silent. Marion felt her ears burning and her face grow hot. Her caramel skin went copper in the sun long ago. She just held her face down towards her plate.

"Stop shoveling all that food in your face," he said.

Marion noticed that everyone on the patio seemed to think the ball was in her court. Why not? A corn-fed black woman was bound to be uncouth in public, wasn't she? It was expected.

Marion ignored Bobby and signaled for the waiter to bring her another glass of water, instead.

40

An elderly gentleman at the next table was having Bobby's exact same breakfast. He caught Marion's eye and gave her an approving nod. She acknowledged but wondered how on earth anyone besides the four of them could have heard the conversation. Most of the patrons were older--even a few with hearing aids. Maybe that was why.

The meal was continued in mostly silence and awkward smiles. Bobby reached for the check—as usual so Marion figured he was just really, really being himself-- except that she had not seen that side of him before.

Niece suggested they walk along the shoreline. They paired off. Tom and Niece ended up in the water, surprisingly with swimsuits. Marion and Bobby kept walking.

"I really didn't appreciate your comments at breakfast. What is your problem with me?" Marion said.

"Usually it's the guy who admits that the relationship is just sex but you went ahead and took that imitative," Bobby said.

Marion stopped walking and cocked her head a bit. She could not believe that man only wanted to shake her confidence—take her down a peg or two for being honest.

"Oh, it's like that. You trying to knock me off my square or something," Marion said. She was gesturing and moving her shoulders and getting loud.

"There you go again acting like a dude." Bobby said. He thought the whole thing was cute but Marion just wasn't in the mood. She was tired of this type of scenario.

"Who the fuck do you think you are? My boyfriend? My man? How dare you approach me like that with that Neanderthal attitude? This ain't no motherfucking Geico commercial. How you gone step to me like that? I have never mistreated you in that way!" Marion said.

She was just talking and talking and screaming and waving her arms in the air like a big old brown ape. Niece and Tom stopped splashing in the water to watch-- along with the other early risers on the beach—Marion's complete emotional meltdown.

Bobby just kept walking backwards and laughing. He was glad to get a rise out of Ms. Proper. Everything had to be just right or her way but now she was out on the beach in her new hometown looking crazy as hell.

Marion turned around to see where her friends were. Nicey was walking toward her, Bobby walking away and Tom was running to catch up with Bobby.

"No, Nicey – just stop by my house when y'all through over here. I'm going home," Marion said, stomping up the sand, arms a swinging—she was almost marching.

Nicey gave up and watched her friend march through the sand. She started to laugh. She had to admit that her friend looked kind of ridiculous stomping off like a little kid. It also showed that she had some kind of emotion tied up in Bobby, even if it was a little more than seething hate right about now.

"I got sand in my hair and shit," Marion said, mumbling.

It was a short walk to her home on the hill but she never had to walk up her own drive. By the time she reached the front door she was wringing wet and crying. She went inside and made herself a drink at the bar. She sat at her own bar, staring into her drink just as if she was at a bar accept that she was sobbing loudly and alone.

The break was a long time coming. She had not cried once through the whole work debacle but she was a little tired and was blindsided by the fool who mocked her in public and unapologetically laughed in her face about it. She thought Bobby would apologize and they'd make up later after spending the day together. There were so many places she wanted to show him in her new hometown. Now, she was just the crazy girl yelling on the beach wringing wet and sitting at her own bar-- alone. She cried some more when she noticed Nicey had not yet knocked on the door to see about her.

Hours passed. No one called or came by. Marion called Nicey on her cell phone. No answer. Marion went up to bed to finish her drink. The silence was deafening. She was even too stubborn to turn on the television. She decided to shower and go out. The opulence and vastness of her own shower mocked her. This kind of display was for happy people—not her.

When she got to the bar—that was supposed to be for Deerfield Estates homeowners-- she sat alone, shoulders slumped. She drained her whiskey glass-- twice. The after-work set didn't have as much zip in her area of the world because there were a lot of start-up kings and queens and they were filthy rich. They traveled and were not a part of the proletariat class.

Locally, her so-called exclusive bar was a little flat. She was going to go until she felt someone standing behind her. Whoever it was standing so close she could feel heat radiating.

"You're too pretty to be here," a man's voice said before she had a chance to turn around. There was also a very big, nicely manicured hand holding her arm. She turned around slowly. It was the handsome Florida State Trooper she met at the gas station.

"I'd never thought we'd run into each other again," Marion said.

"Why not, I gave you my card," he said smiling and showing off the whitest, straightest teeth ever. And he smelled good too. His white shirt was crisp and he was wearing Armani. She looked up into his eyes. He saw her pain as they locked into each other's gaze.

"Hi, I'm Kelly," the handsome man standing next to the trooper said. He broke the mood, sticking his hand out. Marion accepted. Even his friends are cute, she thought to herself.

Gas Station Divas

"I'm sorry, officer, I can't remember..." Marion stammered.

"Ron. I'm Ron Bowling. You can drop the officer part—unless you're breaking the law. Besides, I'm a state trooper. You do look a bit young to be in here," he said.

Marion laughed. Instantly her mood was up. She sat up straight.

"Thank you. How did you know I could use a little pick me up?" Marion said.

Ron hunched his broad shoulders. He had a silly grin on his face. He had managed to block her entire view of the bar and of his friend. It was as if they were the only two in the place.

Ron bought drinks and Marion laughed. She loved his sense of humor. She couldn't believe it. Her day had started out so crappy only to end up so wonderful. She kept looking up into Ron's face. He was lovely and glowing.

His complexion was so smooth and his eyes so friendly and sparkly. He had the longest lashes. Marion reached out and lightly touched her fingertips to his soft wavy hair. Marion liked men with nice hair and nice eyes. She was captivated by his handsome face.

Ron was nice. Marion was a bit tipsy—again and on purpose. She was touching him. When she drinks she touches, Ron thought to himself. He liked it. Marion liked it. Ron was smiling, his hair already sporting specks of silver. Marion had leaned over so far on the barstool that Ron might as well had been holding her up.

"How are we going to get home? Marion asked.

"Why, did you walk up here? You live around here?"

"Yeah, I do but I drove. You won't arrest me, will you?"

"Well... now Kelly can drive my car and I'll drive yours, okay?"

"Okay, but what if I wanted to drive mine?"

"I wouldn't be able to let you do that. I'm sorry miss. Besides, I wouldn't want anything to happen to you on my watch anyways," Ron said.

"Okay good, let's go home. I should be home now—when I'm like this. Shoot, I might have to go look for a job or something and my future boss is in here," Marion said, standing up.

"You need a job, sweetie? You're not working?"

"Actually no, I'm not. I probably shouldn't even be here," she said.

"Well, probably not. How long have you been in Florida?"

"Almost a year."

"And you live around here?""

"Yeah why?"

Ron stood back and looked at Marion. It was funny that her name reminded him of the opera singer, Marion Anderson. He didn't want to tell his age right away so he kept that nerdy factoid to himself but he realized he didn't know this woman very well at all and here he was getting her quite tipsy at the least. He almost forgot he was a law enforcement professional.

43

Gas Station Divas

"It's just that this area is rather exclusive. I figured you were from West Palm Beach or something," he said.

Marion had been in Florida long enough to catch the impact of the officer's statement. She wrinkled her nose and scrunched her face in disapproval.

"Naw, man let's go—you and your friend," Marion said. The alcohol had numbed her just enough to be herself.

The trio marched out of the bar. Kelly was going to drive Ron's car. Kelly brought a friend out of the club with him.

The four of them were floored when Marion pulled up into her long winding and extremely steep driveway.

"You must be widowed," Ron said.

"No child, no. I used to work but let's just say I retired early," Marion said, chest stuck out even farther than usual. They got out of the car and Marion started up to the door.

Kelly pulled Ron to the side.

"Man, isn't this the little Cubana Place? Who you going up in there with man? Do you know this chick?"

"Yeah, she cool, she said she works—or something. Look, either I'll be loving her or arresting her. I'll call if I need backup. She doesn't even know the history of this place and I don't want to be the one to tell her," Ron said, head down and laughing a little.

"Man call me if you need me but me and my date going back to the club," Kelly said.

"I know man, I understand. I'll catch up with you later. Take good care of my shit," Ron said laughing.

"You better tell her man—be a friend," Kelly shouted as he climbed back into his friend's black Land Rover.

Marion was standing on the steps to her cartel-hide-a-way-turned-runt mansion of a home.

"What was all of that about?"

"Kelly works with S.W.A.T. and he has bad memories of this place, that's all," Ron said.

Marion stood on the steps with her hands on her hips.

"What?"

Once settled into the comfort of her home, Ron explained how the former owners had been under investigation for some time and how the Drug Enforcement Administration and the Department of Alcohol Tobacco and Firearms raided the place after the investigation and how there was a little bit of a shootout—years before the house hit the market.

Gas Station Divas

"Oh. Well, I saw some bullet holes had been patched up," she said hunching her shoulders.

"It doesn't scare you to be here--especially by yourself?" He asked.

"No, should it?"

Ron shook his head for no. He didn't want her upset nor did he want her looking for the rest of the electronic listening devices still active in the house. He didn't tell her everything.

Weeks after the raid, one of the DEA agents posted on his blog that they leave the bugs in sometimes as a joke or if they can't find them all or whatever--not expecting average citizens to buy those types of homes.

First off, if another cartel moves in they already have access. If it's a law-abiding private citizen, then it's just for kicks. Florida's history as a hide-a-way for drug activity and fugitives dictate that the Constitution sometimes gets ignored. Kelly told Ron about the blog in passing and he went to it one day when he was tired of looking at porn on the web. He e-mailed the guy and he confirmed it. He even had some audio clips that he e-mailed to Ron. The usually upstanding trooper became fascinated with the private life of the crazy woman who talked to herself. He tracked her down and had been following her—like he does all of the women in which he finds himself interested. Sometimes it ended up in a case and sometimes a good piece of ass—whatever.

In Broward County, a house with that history doesn't sell for that much--as far as home sales go. Marion just happened to be in the right place at the right time—so to speak. She really didn't care who owned it before her, as long as it was hers.

She started to tell Ron about the UPS packages coming there all the time but decided against it. He was still a cop and she always refused the packages.

"I like it here. The previous owners left me an entire bar stocked with liquor. I didn't even find it until this week. I haven't even been through all of the property yet. Matter of fact, I don't know what I've been doing," she said. The Johnnie Walker had settled in and she was officially drunk off of her ass.

The pair went out on the patio to enjoy the quiet swish of the water and to feel the beautiful night air. Marion put her head on his shoulder.

"I like it here," she said.

The pair stayed outside on the comfy patio furniture and fell asleep. They ended up watching the sun come up together.

***

"Why didn't you go in the house?" Ron asked, getting up and stretching.

"I didn't want to spoil it—for once. Want some coffee?"

"Yeah, I do."

Ron smiled that sweet smile at her.

Gas Station Divas

Marion got up and made coffee for them both. While the coffee was brewing she grabbed some loungewear. She saw some sweats in the clean clothes pile.

She handed Ron the sweatpants.

"Thank you. You're very considerate."

Ron followed Marion into the huge master bath.

Damn, this fool lives large, he thought to himself.

Any other man would have been intimidated, he thought as he let the hot water jet onto his body. He turned them on full force. He could do without the steam, though. He thought about the properties he owned and figured he did alright. At least he had a job. Poor Marion. He thought about trying to find the rest of the bugs in her house. She didn't deserve to be treated that way. She was a good girl.

As the pair enjoyed their German coffee, there was a knock at the door. It was Niece, Tom and Bobby. They didn't want to leave without saying goodbye. Marion didn't quite know what to do.

"Well, can we come in?" Niece said.

"Yes, I'm sorry."

Marion swung open the heavy door and let the trio in. She watched Bobby's face for any reaction. He was polite but silent.

"Didn't know you had company--so early," Niece said, grabbing Marion by the arm and pulling her into the kitchen.

"Who is that? We brought Bobby over here to apologize!"

"Girl, give it up because we are not a match okay. He is a fool. I met this nice state trooper at the gas station. We met again at this bar over here," Marion said pointing in the general direction of the bar.

"Isn't he cute? You know, I did call you yesterday. Had you answered the phone, none of this would have happened. So, it's not my fault," Marion said.

"Well as long as you are happy, Marion. Bobby is an asshole. We took him out and he hit on anything that moved in front of him. He was so drunk when we got out of there, girl shoot. You didn't miss a thing," Niece said.

"Where did yall go?"

"Club Blue. I had never been there. Bobby loved it," Nicey said.

"Wow, I'm glad y'all had a nice time but I still have an attitude with Bobby. I guess I didn't know him that well. I didn't even know that I didn't know him that well. I didn't know he could be so mean," Marion said.

The women walked out of the kitchen to find all three men on the patio.

"Well, guys, I see you've met Ron. Ron this is Nicey,"

"Hi," Nicey said with a little wave and a smile.

"I need to talk to you, Marion," Bobby said. His face was expressionless.

Ron frowned and watched them as they walked inside the house.

Gas Station Divas

"Look, I didn't mean for all of that to get out of hand yesterday. We're okay right?" Bobby said.

Why should we be okay? That was really fucked up how you treated me," Marion said.

"I explained it on the beach," he said.

"You are a child, I swear--a child. If we have problems in the future, I would appreciate it if you just tell me what is bothering you. I said what we were doing was just sex because we really don't know each other that well and you had not made any overtures for a serious relationship--like you had other options and stuff so I just let it go and opted for sex. I took the easy way out," Marion said, wiping tears from her eyes.

"I'm sorry," Bobby said. They hugged and Bobby kissed her on her temple. She looked up at him with still teary eyes and he knew at that point how wounded she had been. She was fragile and he stomped on her. Now he was trying to piece her together in the three minutes they had left, while a new dude waited in the wings. He looked at her.

"Who is that dude out there to you?"

"I met him while out one day, why?"

"Did you sleep with him?"

"No, I haven't--not that there would be anything wrong with that. Are you tripping again?"

"Naw, just concerned. Don't be hoppin' into bed with every man you meet. It doesn't matter if he's a cop--that might make it worse," Bobby said. She looked into his eyes and he seemed sincere. Marion decided not to yell at him anymore.

Marion stared at him as he walked away. She was so surprised at his concern-- feigned or real. She watched him walk away and she felt good about them. They were okay.

Marion waved to her friends as she walked them to the car. She purposely left the door open so that Ron could clearly see they were all just friends.

When she returned to the patio, she saw that Ron had refilled their cups with coffee. He had even prepared coffee for her guests. She was impressed. She gave him a kiss and a hug. She put her head on his shoulder.

"What was all of that about," he said in between sips.

"They wanted to visit. Niece and Tom have a South Beach condo."

"Damn, a rich girl with rich friends."

Marion looked up at him. He was smiling. She smiled too.

"Yeah, they're pretty good friends."

"No wonder you're down here," he said.

"What do you mean?"

"They told me about your job—your old job and stuff. That must have been pretty rough," Ron said.

"Why did they tell you that?"

"I asked."

"What did you ask them?"

"I asked them how they knew you—you forget I'm a Hoosier too," he said.

"You cop you. You interrogated my friends about me?" Marion said smiling.

"Un-hunn. I wanted to know. It really wasn't making sense until today. Lots of people come down here to get away from it all. You were kinda looking like a mob moll or something," he said.

"Hooking up with a cop—I'm a mob moll?"

"Well stranger things have happened and lots of women are drawn to police for protection from something—real or imagined. I didn't know what was up."

"Couldn't it be that I just like you? You are attractive—and nice," Marion said.

"Bobby seemed to like you a lot," Ron said, putting the cup to his lips.

The brief silence between them hurt her ears.

"He talked me up? I'm surprised. He and Tom—I swear—take turns getting on my last nerve. I don't see how Nicey puts up with either one of them," Marion said, laughing off the obvious direction of the conversation.

"Umph," Ron said quietly.

"Don't be that way. It's nice, us being here together. I tried to call to hook up with them but they were too busy at Club Blue," Marion said. It still hurt her a little, being ignored and left out.

"I'm tired, let's go lay down. We could watch TV or something. I promise not to touch you," Marion said.

Ron put his coffee cup down and cupped her face. He kissed her soft lips, cheeks and eyes and lips again.

"You've already touched me," he said.

As they walked to the bedroom, he tried to fight feelings that she was a whore and had the taste of some other man on her mouth.

He really liked her. It wasn't right that he should be hurt so soon. Stalking had its disadvantages—like starting a relationship with a person without their knowledge, way before they get to know you.

Gas Station Divas

CHAPTER 8
PHOTO FINISH

Marion scampered around her home as if she were Ron's wife. Over the months, their relationship grew. She gathered Ron's clothes and dropped them off at the cleaners, washed his socks and underwear, made him lunch and even gave him a long back rub and scalp massage.

"Hey, how about after we pick up the dry cleaning we go to my house for a while?" Ron asked.

"Okay. Do you have to work today?" Marion asked.

"I called off. I have vacation days I don't get to use because I guess I never had a reason to call off for an early weekend before now," Ron said.

"Really?"

"Yup. I like you. You feel comfortable—kinda like these sweatpants," he said, laughing.

Marion bit him playfully on his side. He kissed her.

"Soft and warm and dependable," he whispered, kissing her. They were falling in love, he felt—or at least he was. She was a place he really wanted to be. She wasn't from here, wasn't as materialistic, wasn't really wealthy, kind of simple—a lady.

He fought the urge to joke about whose sweatpants he was wearing. He was learning to let things go—the unreasonable thoughts. Therapy was helping. Besides, she had some meat on her—enough for the sweatpants to be hers.

Oh, the love fest that ensued. They were inseparable the entire summer—just like children. He was over her house, she was over his, they ran each other's errands, drove each other's cars and Ron even introduced her to his family. But the dreaded electronic mail was her downfall. She was perfect until Ron had a need to use Marion's computer to check his e-mail.

Normally, that would not have been a problem however, while sitting there he saw a couple of interesting programs. One was her online diary and another was a huge photo file.

One click led to another and before he knew it he was going through her files. He had found the pictures. If the photos had been money he would have hit the jackpot. He thought at first, she liked celebrities and was one of those kooks.

He saw her read the People magazine and the Enquirer at the grocery checkout once and he teased her about it. She played it off with a laugh and they went on. It seemed odd to him that she only had pictures of Nicolas Cage and Seth MacFarlane. The woman must have had well over a thousand of them—all of two pretty white boys. Why them? He couldn't understand. She had several of Cage's movies but they were the really good ones like 8MM, Gone in Sixty Seconds, Face Off, The Rock, Ghost Rider, National Treasure--everybody's collection had those. And she had ordered every one of MacFarlane's DVDs but they were really funny so most adults who watch cartoons had those. The assorted unopened DVDs and VCR tapes were stored in boxes on a shelf in her closet toward the back, as if they were supposed to be hidden. He thought about it a while because she didn't have a DVD player.

He closed the files and got to thinking. He realized he really didn't know that woman from Adam and here he was introducing her to his family and letting her into his home. He also noticed her diary stopped after she met him.

He knew most of what had been going on in her life anyway—since he had been spying on her since she moved into the house but he was fuzzy on the details of her private life she led in Indiana. Her dossier was scarce.

She wasn't a principal player. All he ever did was keep an eye on her whereabouts as it related to her boss Milos. He always felt the Agency made too big of a deal about her anyway but she was cute and it was his job.

All he found out is that she was a spokeswoman for a company in legal trouble and she was offered a lump sum to go away. And he knew that because she and her friends had told him. 'What kind of agent am I,' he thought to himself, shaking his head.

"What are you doing?" Marion said, startling him out of his thoughts.

"Nothing—I had to check my e-mail. You don't mind, do you?"

"Oh no, I don't but it looked as if you were reading my stuff. Don't read my stuff—yet," Marion said.

"I won't."

Ron looked at her. She was comfortable letting him ramble around her home alone. She couldn't have had much to hide. Was she a stalker? God how that would be embarrassing for him to find out she had been stalking some movie star—just like the woman who was stalking Dave Letterman. Just like anyone who had the

Gas Station Divas

misfortune of being the better half of someone accused of a heinous or--in his case--completely embarrassing crime.

"Did you pick a restaurant for tonight sweetie?" Marion said.

"Baby, listen, I have to give you a rain check on the dinner tonight but I will meet you for lunch tomorrow, okay?" Ron said.

She stared at him.

"Why--what happened? Did I do something?" Marion said. She looked as if she had heard the worst news of her life. Her face was all screwed up, standing there with her arms akimbo.

"No, it's some police work—investigations and stuff," he said.

With that excuse, he kissed her on the forehead and the lips. He sure would hate to leave her but he couldn't have that kind of bad press connected to him and keep his job.

Marion saw him move like the wind through her house. He packed up everything he had ever left there. He even took the extra guns she found hidden in a locked box. She knew they were guns but didn't say anything.

"Wait a minute, that stuff has been sitting on that chair all week. Why are you packing up all your stuff like we're breaking up or something?" Marion said, hands on her hips. She moved over to the computer. The photo icon was still highlighted. A cold emptiness sunk into her belly. Her head buzzed. He had found the photos. What should she do? Should she laugh it off or ignore it like he was doing. She would go for the laugh off after the play-it-off.

"Did you get a bad e-mail or something? Marion said.

Marion sat down at her computer. Ron watched her open the photo file.

"Trying to check my e-mail? You don't know my passwords," he said, walking towards her.

"No just looking at my photos making sure you didn't take anything," she said. She was sweating and her stomach hurt like heck.

She could have slammed her forehead into the computer screen and not felt a thing at that moment. Instead, she crossed her legs and leaned into the screen.

"Did you see my collection of Nic and Seth photos?" she said sweetly.

"Uh yeah, I saw it. You really like Nicolas Cage and that other dude, huh?

Marion turned her face up towards Ron's and smiled sweetly, nodding.

"His name is Seth MacFarlane. He writes the Family Guy cartoon and stuff," she said without a hitch. She surprised herself at how calmly she delivered her lines.

Ron looked into her eyes. They were as clear as a bell. She completely delighted in those photos and was willing to share them with him. Share her obsession. She closed the file and hunched her shoulders.

"Doesn't everybody star gaze? They are both hot and Nic's a great actor. Seth writes comedy gold on a regular. I like just about anything Nic's in and the Cavalcade of Comedy had me in tears," she said. Playing it off seemed to be working.

Marion had started to help Ron gather things around the house.

She made it a point to handle the lockbox with the guns in it. He had not asked her permission to bring firearms into her home. Who was he to judge? She did have kids even though they weren't there at the time.

Besides, if she had to crawl around on her knees to get him to stay, she would. She liked him being around so much and he went to work from her house and she stayed at his—they tailored their individual schedules around each other so that they were never apart more than they had to be. It wasn't forced, it was natural. They both wanted to be together.

"Yeah but why do you have so many photos of these men? What are you doing with those photos? Where did you get them? Are you stalking them or something? Marion, I wasn't going to say anything because I know I had no business in your files but what if you found a bazillion photos of Angelina Jolie on my computer or something? What would you think?

"I wouldn't think anything except that you were a fan. Who doesn't like Angelina? What are you getting at, Ron? What's wrong with photos of Nic and Seth on my computer? Are you jealous?"

"I don't know Marion. I never pictured you as some rabid fan—of anything—let alone a movie star and no, I am not jealous. Have you ever spoken to Nicolas Cage or Seth MacFarlane and tried to contact them? And what is with this 'Nic and Seth'?'"

"No—do you know them? Could I meet him?" Marion said, truly happy at the thought but playing her plan to the hilt.

"No, sweetie I don't know any movie stars. I thought you were a stalker Marion, really, I did. I was getting out of here. The last thing I need is some bad press drawn to me. I'm a cop—a Florida State Trooper. I can't date or be with a criminal—besides that it would be distasteful to me personally. In all honesty, I was headed to the station to run a thorough background check on you—nationwide. I don't know much about your life in Indiana. We're from the same state but I saw the pictures—I guess I overreacted, baby I love you I don't want to go. I didn't know what to do. I got to thinking—what else don't I know about you?"

Marion, in her obsession with photos of men she'll never meet, didn't hear immediately what Ron said until after a few minutes. But, she did hear it. He said, "I love you." It was in the middle of an argument but he loves her.

"I'll delete the photos, Ron. I didn't think they were a big deal. I mean I could see if you were Nicolas Cage or Seth MacFarlane and you found them and reacted and all. I guess I'm still a teenager at heart but I will delete the photos."

She sat down and deleted the files to wastebasket, where she could recover them later and put them on a flash drive.

"You didn't have to do that. I was more concerned that you were into some criminal activity or something," Ron said.

"Too late. Now will you stay?" Marion got up and put her arms around his rock hard middle and ran her face up his chest to his neck, nibbled on his ear and then kissed him on the cheek. He felt so good in her arms that it drew tears. She let go.

"All I know is that I better not find your collection of old Jet Magazine centerfolds, Playboys or Hustlers or something," Marion said jokingly.

"They're collectables. I've been collecting Jets since I was a little kid. I still subscribe to the other two but I'll cancel them. Damn, I hadn't looked at it that way baby," Ron said, looking down and feeling foolish. The pair hugged.

"I'm hungry," she said.

"You're always hungry,"" Ron said.

"Can we go eat now?"

"Yes."

"Drinks first?"

"Yes, baby--drinks first!"

Ron kissed Marion and they almost didn't make it out of the house. Besides, what if she goes back into the deleted items folder and download all of her pictures onto her USB and be done with it, he thought. It's not that she really needed them anymore but who could be sure about the future.

He slowly began to put his belongings back as Marion sashayed off to make them drinks by the hot tub. He could see her ass through her robe and it was nice--nice and round like an onion.

However, she was right. What she was doing was no different than what he and other men had been doing for generations with centerfolds, pin-up girls and porn. It was basically the same, maybe less egregious but all the more startling because he had never known a woman to do anything like that. We all obsess over something, thought to himself, why did I overreact? Am I angry that she picks a white actor, a white man, instead of black?

What about the white female's Mandingo warrior fantasy? Black females are certainly out the outside of that, he thought to himself. Then, he thought maybe he overreacted because she had photos of men who were insanely wealthy.

I told her that I loved her. Did she hear me? Maybe not with all of the hollering, he thought to himself. Maybe that is why he overreacted. He hadn't meant to admit that even to himself and didn't want to say it but it was out there. His thoughts were beginning to run together. Ron shook his head at the situation, thinking of how many good friends he had who happened to be white and how shocked they would be if they were privy to the conversation. He really did love her and he really didn't want to let her go. He wanted to be in love. She could be so good for him.

When they got home, Ron and Marion made love for hours. They nearly hurt themselves because neither would go to sleep. It was if they had both discovered precious gold between themselves and they were not let go. It was good for their first time. Ron even liked to cuddle after sex. Marion was in heaven.

The pillow talk was even interesting.

"I remember my first car it was a $5,128 pile of shit--dark blue exterior and crap blue interior. That car had so many mechanical problems... I was overcharged for it. They were selling them outside of the Welfare department from a card table. Two white ladies and a black one.," Ron said, nestling himself into the pillow.

Marion laughed.

The black one knew that what she was doing was unethical, selling those lemons--I could see it in her face when I looked at her. I thought they were social workers--I trusted them. The sad part is that I bought the same crap car twice. I just think I could have gotten a better car for the amount of money I paid.

The office was over there on Homan Avenue. Really--they would not put the numbered address on the clear plastic promotional stickers that each car owner needed to get their piece of crap serviced--that's how crappy the cars were. I had to beg and sweet talk one of the stickers from the one of the ladies. They knew the cars they sold were crap but they had a job to do. I was just another sucker to them.

Marion was stunned. This wasn't the type of pillow talk she was used to but she liked it because it was coming out of Ron's mouth.

"What were you doing at the Welfare office in Chicago?

"It's a long story, for another time," Ron said, kissing Marion on the mouth.

"Did you keep the car?"

"Yes, I did Marion.

Gas Station Divas

CHAPTER 9
SPLISH SPLASH

In the quest to keep her man, Marion almost forgot about her children. She always had wanted to get them a new daddy but it wasn't exactly like getting a new piece of furniture or a pair of new shoes.

The children's old dad had problems of his own and wives of his own. He seemingly had forgotten about her and the kids.

Marion refused to degrade their dad to them because half of him was in them and she didn't want her children to ever feel bad about themselves because they were from a broken home.

Ron seemed to not mention her children. Maybe it was just a summer fling for him she thought but he introduced her to his family. She couldn't figure it out. She promised herself she wouldn't bring her children down there until she secured a job.

Her plan was that when Ron was at work, she would job hunt.

She thought of getting a head hunter but decided to try the old-fashioned way first.

*****

Sitting in the lobby of her potentially new employer really wasn't the time to be thinking about family issues. She tried to focus on her qualifications. Being a good mommy or girlfriend didn't count.

The receptionist gave her the signal.

"Here I go. Back straight, shoulders, smile and walk," Marion thought to herself as she strode into a board room.

Ten minutes later, she strode out.

She nodded to the receptionist with her Colgate smile and walked as if all eyes were on her, even though there was no one else around. She did that all the way to the car—remembering to sit down butt first.

Marion didn't relax until she was on the highway headed 95-South.

She decided to spend the rest of the morning enjoying her slice of the beach. The water was warm. It was so warm it reminded her of bathwater. The saltwater floated her tired body at a steady but slow pace. Laying straight back in the water and looking up at the overcast sky, she thought about her current situation. It was alright but she was getting sick of not working.

She had been working since she was 16 years old. Earning money was the only way she knew. She wasn't from the streets but living off of the interest meant she needed to budget. She needed to prepare for the children because at the end of the summer comes school. And then there was hurricane season. She needed to make special arrangements for her daughter, who is autistic. Her health concerns come first and she'd need a special needs shelter.

She'd check on that after her swim, she thought. She looked around her because the water was beginning to feel cool. The people on the beach looked like colorful dots. She rolled over and began to swim back to shore.

Besides, she left all of her stuff on her towel. Hiding keys and a cell phone in her shoe didn't count as security.

When she reached her blanket, she saw Ron had called.

"Yes, my dear how may I help you today?"

"By having dinner with me. I think there are some things we should discuss."

"Is it serious? I-I-mean did I do something wrong?"

"Did you?"

"No."

"Ron."

"I'm just playing with you, calm down but I do think we need to work out some details about our future together, don't you?"

"Yes."

"Why did you pick that bathing suit to wear? It's the same color as your skin. You look naked. I see now I'm going to have to go through your closets and stuff..."

Marion looked around. He was sitting in a squad car talking on the cell. She ran up to meet him. Besides she wanted all of the women—and some men--on the beach to know that Ron was her man. And she really looked good wet.

"How did you know I was here?"" Marion said.

"I guessed and I stopped by."

Marion was hanging inside his car like a badge bunny. Her wet breasts a-jiggle for all of the world to see--and for Ron to see.

"I love you so much," Marion said.

Gas Station Divas

It just came out. She didn't mean to say it because she wasn't thinking she was just feeling. It felt good to hold on to her man like that.

"I love you too baby."

Kiss, kiss, kiss and kiss. They kissed—for all of the world to see.

"But I gotta go."

The radio was squawking out all kinds of codes and siren noises.

"I gotta learn those codes one day. Be careful baby," Marion said.

He waved as he pulled away.

Ron saw that she stood watching him drive away. He put his sirens and lights on. He felt good. He knew exactly where she was. He though it strange she didn't mention that she had an interview.

Maybe she didn't feel good about the outcome. He'd ask her tonight.

Marion turned around and saw that a few people were watching. She smiled and waved at them. They smiled back with approving nods.

She gathered her things and headed home. Whilst soaking in her antique soaking tub, Marion likened herself to a woman who had chosen shoes that, although beautiful, hurt like hell. She seemed to have it made, if you were looking from the outside inward. She slid down in the tub so the hot water could heal her neck. A wave slapped hard against the back of her head and neck of her while she was in the ocean. It felt like whiplash.

CHAPTER 10
LET'S GET MARRIED TODAY

Marion took the time to wax everything after the soak. She put on her silk lounger and sexy house shoes. It didn't matter that they cost $70—they were still house shoes.

She didn't take the time alone to look at anything on her computer because she finally had the real thing. She figured if Ron was serious he'd eventually ask about her family. She missed her children. She heard the doorbell.

"Hey, boo," Marion said. She kissed Ron like it was their first kiss. He looked so good and rugged—like the Marlboro man or something. She couldn't yet put her finger on it.

"Like it?" Ron said, holding out his arms. He was decked out in black police gear complete with tactical bulletproof vest and straps and sub machine gun, pistol and body armor equipment.

"I went on an operation. It felt good to get back, I dunno, into the swing of things. I look good, don't I?""

"You look good. What do you mean back into the swing of things?"

"Well I really don't plan to keep going on operations. I'm a little old for that. I was just helping out today. That's where I was going when I saw you at the beach. I wanted to see you before I went there."

"Reliving your youth huh," Marion said, kissing him. She walked toward the bedroom.

She misses every opportunity I take to express my feelings about us, he thought as he walked toward the bedroom.

He started taking off his gear not because he anticipated sex but because it was hot and heavy. The tactical gear weighed at least 40 pounds. And the boots were hot. A midnight dip in the ocean wouldn't be a bad idea. He was glad Marion lived near the ocean. They could walk there and talk. Maybe the brightness of the moon and the sound of the ocean would relax her and open her up. The only time she seemed to relax was after sex and then she went to sleep.

"Did you get that job you went for?" Ron said, breaking the silence.

"I don't know yet. I doubt it. Durable Medical gave a good reference I'm sure but how good of a reference can they give? They have their own problems," Marion said.

"True. Do you plan to stay here Marion—I mean when will you send for your children? I'd like to meet them at least."

Marion sat on the bed.

"Yeah, we should probably talk about that," she said.

Ron continued to take off his gear, secured his guns in the lockbox he kept on his side of the bed and slid one under the pillow. He couldn't help it. He knew Marion didn't like guns but he was a cop—what did she expect?

Ron looked over at Marion. She was looking at her toes. They were manicured—nice too. She kept herself up.

"Well?"

"What do you want to know Ron?" You're from Gary, Indiana too. You know what it's like there. I mean, Richard Hatcher isn't in office anymore. Scott King was mayor for 10 years and then Rudy Clay was elected and shortly after that I left for here," Marion said rather matter-of-factly.

"What is the matter with you woman? You know what I'm talking about and it's not politics. Where do I stand? What are we doing here? Are we just fucking or what?"

"And I'm from Hammond!""

"I don't know what to tell you about it. I don't want us living together with the kids in the house but we can continue to be boyfriend and girlfriend," she said.

She never stopped grooming herself and gazing into the mirror. Now she was brushing her hair. It was as if they were discussing where to eat dinner.

"I don't need to live with you," Ron said exasperated. He took off his combat boots and socks, getting madder and madder.

He walked around to Marion's side of the bed.

"What do I have to do? Okay, marry me Marion. Let's get married—I'm serious," Ron said, staring into her eyes to see some kind of emotion. He saw fear. She looked like a dear caught in the headlights of a Mac truck.

"Okay, you want to marry me?" Marion said.

Gas Station Divas

"Yes, I want to be here with you. I come here after work. I can't think about us not being together. I don't want us to be apart. We get along. I can actually get along with you. That's major!

Ron got down on one knee.

"I don't have a ring right now but marry me. Say yes please."

"Yes, Ron I will marry you. I love you. Thank you."

This woman actually said 'thank-you,' Ron thought to himself.

Marion threw her arms around his neck and kissed him all over his face. She was grinning from ear-to-ear.

"You have such a beautiful smile," Ron heard himself say.

"Now we can go home to meet my parents," Marion said pulling her man into bed.

"Is that what you were waiting for—a proposal?" Ron said.

"Yes. I didn't know what to do. I didn't want to pressure you into anything you didn't want to do so I kept it light and breezy. And it worked.

"You'd be really good at poker. I couldn't read you for a minute there. You acted as if you could care less—like a dude. Sucking up all the sex and the gifts—and stuff. You had me going for a minute," Ron said.

"What was I supposed to do, propose to you?" Marion said.

"You could have," Ron said.

"You wouldn't have respected that. That doesn't even sound like you," Marion said.

"Yeah, you're right. It would have freaked me out. I do love you, by the way—really."

"I know. Thank You. I love you too."

Marion started to take off Ron's shirt and unbuckle his belt but Ron was still talking.

"When will we go see your parents and get the kids? Don't you have to enroll them in school?"

"Yeah, I do." Marion stopped for a minute and thought about all of the things she would have to do to get everything back on track. She laid her head on Ron's chest. She could hear his heart beating. It was so soothing. She wrapped her arms around him. She knew she needed him but she was scared. He had everything in his life under control and knew what he was doing and where his future would lead him. She had none of that and was afraid to let him see how little control she had in her life. It was embarrassing.

"Ron, I know you think I have my stuff together but I don't. I'm just putting on appearances. This is the best I have done for myself thus far. The only thing I knew is that I had to get out of Gary. Things were unraveling fast."

"Are you in some kind of trouble?""

Gas Station Divas

"No, not really—I guess," Marion said. She ran down everything that had been going on in her life before she became the proud owner of her new house.

Marion was broke as hell until she got that job with Durable Medical. On and off of welfare and constantly in between writing jobs, no editor had wanted to be bothered with her and her instinct for news. Watergate was over and the type of journalism she had learned to write at Indiana State had seen its time come and go. Matter of fact, she figured the J profs at ISU had taught them all of that stuff—real news reporting—as a joke on the world. They taught what they knew— digging for the truth, 1940s style. They were getting back at a world that had spit in their faces just for doing their jobs. One of her professors had actually been a muckraker of the 1940s and actually wore a press card in his hat. That was when blacks didn't even make the news let alone work for news agencies—mainstream anyway. Back then blacks were invisible except to other blacks. Blacks had their own presses.

However, the whole industry changed and had been taken over by big business starting in the late seventies. Advertisers, businessmen and politicians were the shot callers, not editors, reporters and publishers. After all, reporters had to live in the world they report about and it's not that hard to find out where a person lives.

Marion had rubbed plenty of people the wrong way with her stories about dead prostitutes, runaway kids, gentrification—the way blacks are treated behind the blue line—F.O.P matters—F.B.I. matters--you name it and she had written something about it. Her worst mistake was writing about prosecutorial misconduct. Who has the balls to throw rocks at local government?

She got a pass because she was green and thought she was doing some good. So, they sent her hometown to do some good.

It was fine for a while. Marion learned how to write a decent feature story instead of the hard news she was used to writing but as time went on, writing jobs became scarce. Freelancing worked for her then when she had two babies and a husband. But James couldn't take her being a reporter. He was working most of the time but Marion was in the constant company of high-powered men. It was too much and he left on a Super Bowl Sunday--walked right out of the door—no hard feelings. She knew it was coming so it didn't hurt as much as it could have.

As head of her own household, the freelancing was only enough money to keep a roof over her head but after her beloved editor Leslie Chetfield died, so did the news in Northern Indiana. No wonder he had a heart attack because he was single handedly holding up all of the news reporting for an entire city.

His death really affected Marion. She didn't know quite what to do. Durable Medical was her saving grace but it too was short lived. Marion really didn't want to have to share all of that with Ron. He seemed to like her so much and she didn't want to ruin it. Besides, there were some things she had to leave out for her and his sanity.

Besides, the issue of her parents was enough in and of itself. The kids were such brats sometimes but what can you expect from brats but brat behavior. They spoiled her and tried to keep her in check but wild-ass Marion had ideas and plans and just had to go to Florida.

She interviewed for the National Inquirer once and stayed in Boca Raton a week. She fell in love with the pastel buildings and the wealth that surrounded her. When she returned without being hired, she continued with her local freelance writing. Her parents didn't want her to move permanently to Florida with the children—they thought she should have a man to help her with that so they struck a compromise. She was to leave the children with her parents until she gets herself set up.

Now, she is set up and in love and about to be married.

How would they take that?

She wondered if Ron would automatically know what all else went along with what she told him. He really was listening, it seemed. No one can come out of a situation like that unscathed. Marion was given over to panic attacks and had really taken to being indoors mostly. She wasn't as outgoing as she had once been. She partied a lot in Chicago and sometimes in Gary—mostly at a cop bar her friend Toni told her about. Ron didn't have to know everything. He might think her to be a badge bunny or groupie or something like that because she only hung out with a certain type of individual.

But, at least he listened.

"Well. That's not so bad. I mean, I'm here for you. I'd make an excellent father—if you would have that," he said.

Marion cocked her head to the side wondering was she really that selfish and that bad of a mother. Here she was blathering on about how her life is affected and Ron's main concern was her children and how they would be raised with him in the picture. The kids were just along for the ride in her mind. Her parents would have better insight into this anyway. She really depended on them.

"I know you will, baby." Marion said.

"And our baby will be just as nice. You think you got a couple more in ya?" Ron said smiling.

"Huh, you wanna see me pregnant? No. Nooooo."

"So, is that a deal breaker?"

"No there are no deal breakers unless you're abusive or something. There are no deal breakers but you know how I act when it's that time of the month?

"Yeah." "Magnify that by 10 and add crying and more mood swings and fat—much more fat.""

"Not with me around. I'll take care of you. You won't have an unmet need and I won't let you get fat—am I fat?

Gas Station Divas

"No." Marion said, looking at him to see if he was serious. He was. Ron kissed her on top of her head.

He scheduled some vacation time a week later so that they could fly in and meet her parents.

CHAPTER 11
THE BLACK TORNADO

Both of them brought reading material for the flight so they flew in silence. Ron talked Marion out of driving up to Indiana from Florida because he didn't think he'd make the trip in one piece.

Halfway through her book, Marion looked over at Ron. She thought she'd get one really good last look in case the visit didn't go well. He very well may not speak to her again or at least for a very long time. There was so much she didn't tell him and she couldn't imagine what tidbit her parents would let out of the bag. She hoped they wouldn't pull out those photographs—she wanted to stay as far away as possible from that subject.

For instance, he didn't know that her parents were well off. They had hit the lottery for $314 million dollars several years back and decided to take the installments in annual payments—against everyone's wishes.

They refused to move but instead bought the property to the West of them and expanded their existing home. They bought the house next to that one to make sure everyone had space. Mother made decorating it her pet project over the years. They deserved the cash after years of working and struggling but they didn't mind sharing their good fortune. Marion knew she had the best parents a child or adult could have but she couldn't shake the notion that they were sorely disappointed in her outcome. The first time her father actually acted as if he was proud of her is when she turned up pregnant with her daughter. He beamed ear-to-ear as she stood there before him unmarried and scared in their living room with a dress the dry cleaners had destroyed. The snug fitting high-waisted elastic portion of the dress hung loosely— with more than enough room for her expanding belly. They were happy to have their first grandchild while they were still young enough to enjoy her. It didn't hurt that Tonya was cute with big beautiful eyes-- she looked like her dad. Even though Marion and James finally got married (Tonya was in the first grade) and had another child, Marion was still unhappy. Prior to her pregnancy she had wanted to join the Peace Corps. Instead, the toughest job she ever got to have was being mother of two and then a single mother of two.

Her parents were very hard-working people with a no-nonsense approach to life and all of that money had not changed them. Marion figured Ron would like that. What he also didn't know is that Marion well could have just sponged off of her parents forever but she didn't want to—she wanted her own life where she called the shots. And being a shot caller is hard work where you sometimes suffer from your mistakes.

Marion insisted they stay in a hotel. She wanted some kind of privacy. Her parents ruled their home with an iron hand—just like the USSR but pre-wall.

"Are you sure your parents don't want us to stay with you?" Ron said, handing the bell hop some bills.

"No, do you want me to pay half,"" Marion said, reaching into her bag.

"No, that's not the point. Look, I have money—lots of it—okay. It's not that. You know what I have noticed about you? You are very stand-offish and sometimes very unemotional."

Marion sighed and looked away from him. She walked instead over to the Starbucks and got a venti coffee-of-the day Sumatra and then headed over to the bar.

"One shot of Crown, please."

The bartender brought her a beautifully handcrafted dark glass mug and a full shot glass.

"You want me to leave the bottle?"""

Marion smiled finally and shook her head for no.

"You want some of this? She poured half of the cream and coffee out into the glass, replaced the lid and slid it to Ron.

Marion poured the shot into her mug and gulped half of it piping hot or not.

"Are you nervous?"

"Yes"

"Why—they're your parents Marion. I'm the one who should be nervous,"

"I never told them that we would be in town Ron. I didn't have the strength to negotiate or bargain with them nor did I want to have to answer the same questions over and over about my plans for the future. They don't necessarily want me in Florida. They don't even believe I have a house there, man!"

"Oh, I see. You're still scared of your parents, aren't you?"

"Yeah," Marion nodded as she took another long sip of her homemade Irish coffee. She lit up a cigarette and pulled hard.

"I don't know what to tell you kiddo. I've been grown for a long time. I can't tell you that last time my parents scared me. Alcohol isn't going to help."""

65

Gas Station Divas

"The hell you say." Marion fished around in her purse and shook a pill out of the bottle and knocked it back.

Ron gazed at her in amazement.

"I guess you want me to see this side of you. You were always so self-confident and above-it-all."

"Now, you know. It was all an act. I was acting. I probably should have become an actor," Marion said, sucking up the last of her coffee and then starting in on Ron's.

"Look Ron, sometimes I can be on and sometimes I'm like this. With the flight and all—I don't know. Just let me get my legs back and figure out how I'm going to play all of this. There is bound to be some fireworks. I told you they don't even believe I have a home in Florida. They actually thought I'd eventually be coming home for good," Marion said.

"What's wrong with Florida? Why don't they like Florida?"

Marion hunched her shoulders and looked at him. She slowly shook her head. She got on the cell phone and called home to give her mom some kind of warning about the tornado that was about to engulf their lives.

Gas Station Divas

CHAPTER 12
BIG PIMPIN' HILLBILLIES

Pulling up to the house was the first step. It was huge and mother still had plans for more. It was the biggest house on the street. There were five bedrooms in all and five bathrooms. Marion's parents insisted that everyone have their own bathroom— even though they were the only adults in the house.

So that meant no one really had to share bathrooms anymore. Marion's two children had adjoining bathrooms, her brother Larry's children had an adjoining bath and then there was a bathroom for the nursery where Larry's other two children slept when Larry and his wife Marsha were out-of-town.

The other bathrooms were for guests or her parents. Dad used all of them because he said he paid for them. Marion grew up pre-lottery where one bathroom did for the four of them.

They were all spoiled. No longer did they recognize the olden days when they had to wait their turn and share.

He had called Marion's father Mr. Anderson. He didn't realize Anderson was Marion's married name. She kept it so that she and the children could seem like a family, however fractured. Marion's dad frowned at him.

Ron lost his nerve and excused himself to the nearest bathroom.

Marion's father Dave, was something of a character. He loved a good laugh but *he* picked the funny moments. A harebrained scheme to move to Florida wasn't funny to him.

Marion found Ron and tried to persuade him to come out of the bathroom. Her father saw the car and started to look for them in the house. Marion still had keys to her parents' house. Dave knew they were in there but he stopped to listen to the voice mail anyway.

"What do you mean you've come to get the kids?" Marion's father boomed through the kitchen.

"Who is that man?" Dave said.

"That's my fiancé." Marion said.

"Fiancé? Where's your ring?" her dad said.

Marion held out her hand and the flash of the clear, faceted rock amazed her dad.

"Aww, shit. That's not an engagement ring. I got your mother something bigger that that last Christmas. The lady told me it was a cocktail ring.

Marion dropped her arm to her side like a weight.

"Dad, it's clearly an engagement ring. It's a solitaire and it's pretty," Marion said, lip stuck out and clearly, no longer proud of herself.

Marion's dad was silent for a moment.

"Where'd you meet him?"

"In Florida."

"Florida—what's wrong with you? You barely know him and you expect to take these kids away from here down to a land that you don't know anything about with a man you don't know..."

Dave stopped hollering for about a second. It was long enough for him to notice that Ron was still in the bathroom. Marion's mother was mysteriously not there so she had to face the music alone.

"What is he in there doing—taking a dump? Who comes to someone's house and craps? What kind of a man is he?"

"He's actually a Florida State Trooper dad, geeze. And he's from Indiana."

"He can afford that type of ring on a cop's salary?" her dad asked.

Marion rolled her eyes and let out a deep sigh. She was beginning to think about some Black Label and some VSOP.

He owns land in Florida too, dad."

Marion sat down and took a load off. She saw the coffee pot still on.

"How long has this been here?"

"We don't change. You can get two days out of one pot of coffee. We don't change," Dave said, finally sitting down quietly to his Sun-Times newspaper—a constant in the Jones' household.

Luebell and David Jones are a couple. They had been married over 40 years and Dave was right—they had not changed.

Marion laughed a little and poured herself some day-old coffee not missing an opportunity to dump spoonfuls of sugar and creamer in it. She wondered when her mother would get back.

"I gotta take the truck out to Sears later on for a check-up after I go get the kids," Dad said.

Marion guessed even her dad at his age could get a little embarrassed from all of the yelling. Ron was still in the bathroom. It was going on twenty minutes.

"What's wrong with him—he got a drug habit or something?"

Gas Station Divas

Marion lowered her head and laughed.

"No dad."

"What's wrong with him?"

"I don't know. He was talking a lot of mess on the way up here. I thought cops were used to situations. I tried to tell him how you were," Marion lied.

"He's crazy. Now, why would anyone stay in the bathroom that long—especially if they're in town meeting people for the first time?"

"Dad, you're right we haven't been acquainted that long but he's decent and he's a cop and he treats me nice—and he's a land owner so he's not broke. It was his idea to meet y'all and the kids. I didn't tell him you all were rich. I figured he should just find out from the horse's mouth so-to-speak. Now, he knows."

"Knows what?"

"How you guys are—with all of the yelling. And the money,"

"We ain't rich. Shiiiiiit. We just doing alright,"

"Okay Jed Clampet," Marion said exasperatedly taking a sip of her coffee.

"Ellie May." Her dad nodded good-day to her and tipped his baseball cap and laughed as he headed outside.

"Too bad your room was demolished. Now it's part of the kitchen. We do have an extra room up there if y'all staying," her father said.

"We got a hotel room dad," Marion said.

"Why?"

"What do you mean, 'why?' "

Marion could feel her face get hot.

"I'm grown! We're in town and we got a hotel room. I thought you said you had to go get the kids from school?"

Marion's dad laughed. He laughed at her and Ron all the way to the truck. He immediately called his wife.

"Uhh Luebell, you can go back home now. I know you left because you were dodging them. I'm going to go get the kids and then we're going out to Sears," Dave said holding his cell phone like it was a two-way.

"I thought they wanted to take the kids home with them, Dave? Aren't you stopping their plans?

"Who cares? Those two knuckleheads talking about getting married."

"Marion is getting married again?"

"Yep. I didn't see no ring though. Dude wouldn't even come out of the bathroom.

"Ooooh Dave. Did you act a fool?"

"Shiiit. That's my house. She shouldn't have married someone who is scared. Ain't nothing to be afraid of," Dave said sucking his teeth.

"You aught to be ashamed Dave."

"Hey Luebell where are you?"

69

Gas Station Divas

"The Salvation Army."

"Doing what?"

"Trying to see if they'll come get those gold chairs I bought. They don't fit with the new interior."

"Alright. Bye. Hey—don't leave those two up in the house by themselves too long."

Luebell had become exasperated.

"Bye Dave. Don't nobody want nothing in there. She still has her door key. She'll lock up."

"Bye."

The pair hung up and went on about their day as if Marion and Ron had not even come into town.

Marion stood outside of the bathroom door.

"You know Ron, had we taken the road trip we'd only be in Tennessee by now."

"Is you dad gone?" Ron asked, annoyed.

Marion rolled her eyes. It was time for another smoke. She felt like a fish out of water here because she couldn't use her old bedroom as a hideout because it now was a quaint little corner of the enormous kitchen. Mom even had Internet set up for the children. They had also added a screened patio—something Marion had told her mom about over and over again.

"Yeah, he's gone. He went to go pick up the kids from school," she said.

Ron came out of the bathroom.

"Your dad's kinda mean," Ron said.

"He's not mean. He doesn't like change and we're full of change," Marion said. She kissed Ron.

"Oh so you don't mind kissing the scaredy cat?"

"No, not my scaredy cat," she said.

They held each other for a while.

"You didn't tell me your parents were wealthy. How'd your dad make his money. Or your mom?"

"My dad toiled in the steel mills all of my life to put me through college. My brother too if he had he wanted to keep going."

"You all have all of this from a steelworker's salary? Union wages are good but are they this good?"

"After dad retired, he and mom hit the lottery for over $314 million USD. And it's their money—not mine. They do share quite a bit though," she said.

"No wonder you're not worried about a job," he said.

"No, I wouldn't have to worry about that if I lived in Indiana. I, or rather we, live in Florida however. I need to get a job just to make myself feel secure because I never want to run out of money. I sent money to them for the kids—they're not playing around. They don't want me to take the kids to Florida. That's why I put this off as long as I did. Now, I've waited so late that school has started. We start early here in Indiana. I forgot" Marion said, shaking her head at the situation.

"We might as well go back to the hotel. Mom's gone shopping probably. Dad is going to take the truck to Sears and he's taking all of his grandchildren with him. Mom probably has the babies—her and my grandmother. They will be gone until they think we have left. Trust me. Let's go for a swim or something. We're going to have to wait them out," Marion said.

Ron didn't really understand what Marion was talking about but he wanted to get into the isolation of a nice, clean hotel room and some television as soon as possible.

"Oh, so if we act like we don't care they'll make us take the children. I get it—reverse psychology."

"Yeah, it still works. I remember one time when I was in college mom accused me of using psychology on them." Marion said hunching her shoulders and laughing.

"So, your dad's gone to get the kids?"

Marion nodded.

"Do you want a tour of the house?" She asked.

"No, let's go for that swim. Hey—you still have a key to your parent's house?

Marion pulled out her keys jangling them. They locked up the house and went to the hotel.

At least we look good, Marion mumbled, re-adjusting her strappy sandals before heading to the car.

"Oh yeah, I forgot to mention this, my father was elected Mayor last year as well," Marion said, clip clopping down the stairs.

Ron stood there, astonished. He thought to say something but decided he had enough for the day and let it go. Marion seemed to love shocking him with bits of information.

"Really? How nice it must be for him and the city," he said, with a strained smile pasted on his face.

Gas Station Divas

CHAPTER 13
THE SPY THAT LOVES

As soon as they got back to the hotel, she called her parents again and arranged to leave with the children on Monday. She sent for their school records before she left Florida and had private schools already lined up for both of her children. Both schools also had boarding options. If things did not go well between her and Ron, she might have to leave the country for a while. Kicking around Europe, Great Brittan and France couldn't hurt.

That was actually Marion's plan B—leaving the United States behind for a few months.

She knew she would have to start her own business and for her line of work, anyone could become her customer. She wasn't limited by borders—however, she could be limited by her family, friends, fiancé and children.

She flat out told Ron she was going downstairs to the bar. He barely recognized her absence as he stared off into Sports Center.

She felt so tired and a shot of whiskey would not help at all but it would numb her tongue from talking so much. What she really wanted to do is cry.

She sat at the bar alone nursing a drink. There was no one around and it was if she were invisible.

Her phone rang. It was Nicey.

"Whatcha doin'?"

"Nothing, down at the bar."

The women were silent.

"What bar? Where are you?"

"I'm at home—well, in Gary at the hotel. Ron and I came to pick up the kids."

Wait—'Ron and I' –you sound like you guys are serious. Are you two heading down the aisle soon?" Nicey said jokingly.

"Yeah, we are."

Again, silence.

"Wait—you are getting married when?"

"I don't know we haven't set a date yet and we have only been together for a short while, so..."

"Yeah, I know. Girl what are you doing?"

Nicety was almost screaming into the phone. She couldn't believe Marion was turning a summer love into marriage.

"Hello?"

"Yeah, I'm still here—down at the bar."

"Wait there, I'm on my way. Where are you staying?

"We're at the Radisson.""

"We're? Arrrrrrgh. I can't believe that you wouldn't call me about this. I'm calling Toni and Sheila."

Nicety hung up. Within the hour all three women had tracked her down at the bar, still nursing that same drink and looking depressed. She didn't even hear them clattering up the tile walk to the bar area.

The hotel was fabulous—complete with three pools and two waterfalls. She could have gone for a swim to relax.

"Let me see the ring," Toni said, startling her back to reality as the women climbed onto the tall stools.

Marion sheepishly raised her left hand up to reveal the glimmer of the clear rock. All of the women gasped at the five-carat stone, antique platinum setting.

"I got him a diamond pinky ring. I wanted him to have an engagement ring too," Marion said sheepishly.

The women's' mouths were still agape.

"I can't believe this—you're getting married!" Toni said. She and Sheila jumped up and down with the excitement. Nicey just looked at her with a strange look on her face—as if she were afraid for Marion.

"You didn't tell me until tonight so I know you haven't told Bobby. Girl, don't invite him to the wedding," Nicey said.

She shook her head as she grabbed a stool and ordered a drink.

Toni and Sheila bickered about whether or not they should grab a table or get some appetizers.

"What's wrong with y'all?" Sheila said to both Nicey and Marion.

"Well, my problem is that me and my man had a bit of an argument and now he is in the room mad. I think all of this is a bit much for him. He met mom and dad today."

The women screwed up their faces and said "ewwwww."

"How'd that go with your dad and all?" Toni said.

"The usual ladies, the usual. They both showed their natchal asses-- girl their *natchal* asses," Marion said, and burst out in her trademark loud, definitely unladylike guffaw—clapping her hands together and all as she told the story. It was the first time she had laughed all night.

The women grabbed a table and laughed and slapped hands and a-men'ed and order drinks all night. They all threw wedding suggestions at her and debated who would host the bridal shower.

Marion wondered who the stranger at the bar was because he had been staring all night and on the phone.

"Now what is she doing?"

'Nothing Ron. "Laughing. She keeps looking over at me. I think she knows who I am."

"My goodness, Chad, she's never met you. Go talk to her."

"Shiit, I'm not going over there with those cackling hens. Besides, I can read lips pretty well and your girl just referred to me as 'that motherfucker ova thaarr.' Now they are all turning around."

"Okay, just stay cool, stop looking at them and then come back up to the room."

"Okay, by the way congratulations. She's a pretty girl—seems kinda mean but pretty," Chad said.

"Yeah, thanks man, I like her."

"Umhmn and you don't trust her. What's up with that? How are you going to marry her and you don't trust her? Shit you probably don't trust her because you don't know her that well.

"How long have you known her?"

"We met in uhh, March."

"Last year?"

"No, this year. We're up here to meet the parents and stuff."

"Are you marrying her for her money or what dude? You've known her six months!"

"No! I have my own money. Please tell me you are on your way up here and not still sitting down there. She doesn't know I spy on her."

"Apparently. Dude I'm on my way home. I'm not coming up there. You're acting like a little bitch. You better think about this."

"I'm going to marry her. I love her."

"Well, then why did you ask me to come all the way over here to spy on her in the hotel lounge? I live in Wheaton and this is all the way over in Indiana. You should be down here meeting her friends. As long as I've known you, I've only seen this side of you once before."

"Chad no, I feel bad enough now. Don't bring that up."

"You were the only cadet to freak out over your first dead body."

"It was half a corpse. She had been bitten in half by an alligator and had begun to rot in the hot Florida sun. Anyone would have freaked out."

"You fainted dude. And you shitted on yourself a little—I swear!"

"Alright, gross ass. Enough of the memory lane stroll-down. I guess I'll see you at the wedding."

"And when will that be?"

Next year sometime. We have yet to plan it."

"Alright, see ya then."

"Bye."

Gas Station Divas

CHAPTER 14
SPRING WEDDINGS AND OTHER CLICHES

The months just rolled by. Ron and Marion moved in together. They made up. They forgot lots of arguments. They remembered the nights and days they spent making love. They played with the kids. Ron almost told her everything but he didn't. We all know, almost don't count.

Marion got bored easily and Ron was over stimulated, so to keep herself sane, Marion began to plan her own business to fill in the gaps--and to keep her mind off of his job when he was away. She didn't want to worry but she was new at being a cop's wife-to-be and sometimes worried. She loved him so much and it came out in all kinds of ways. She said 'I love you' every time she woke him with a nuzzle and a kiss, and the way she looked at him as he walked through the door. Ron felt her love and appreciated the life they were beginning to make together. He thought the business would be a good idea. Maybe she'd make little trinkets and he'd get his buddies to buy them and she'd be happy finally. She never really seemed completely happy or completely satisfied and it bothered him. He should be all she needed.

But she had this idea for a radio show—except that it wasn't on the radio, it was on the Internet. Ron at first thought, she was just goofing around until one of his friends asked him about it. He had to say, he didn't know because he hadn't heard the show. When he did finally listen, he didn't know what to say. He thought Marion wanted a business and felt her being an Internet radio host personality wasn't a good fit. She had a screechy little voice. But the more he listened the more he was strangely attracted to it. He actually wanted to hear what she would say next. But, the point of any business was to make money. That meant she would have to sell advertising. Everyone knows in sales; the saleswoman sells herself. And knowing Marion she would have accounts based on sex appeal.

Who could want to advertise on her show that didn't want a shot of ass?

"I have two show sponsors so far. That's pretty good. I can build a whole brand on this. Do you like?"

Yeah, he did like. She had sponsors, professional sounding commercials and guests who weren't boring. She wasn't boring. She was actually pretty good at being who she was—a nut—a truthful nut but a nut nonetheless. And yet she was so happy.

Ron was happy for her but wondered where this newest diversion would lead.

Marion saw that he was just staring at her, like he was about to cry almost. She was such a fuck-up but she couldn't figure out what she had done this time. Maybe it was everything all together.

"You know, I never wanted to end up like this—the way that I am. I know that I can be a chore sometimes. I really don't mean to be. I'm sorry about the way I was when we went up North." Marion finally said.

She was a conglomeration of feelings and actions. Clip-clopping clumsily sometimes through life but she finally met someone who accepted or at least put up with that part of her.

Ron never wanted to fix her. He wanted to love her. It was difficult getting through to all of her—the her that got in the way of herself, of life and the her that ignored the obvious.

Ron told her one time if she had a plank of wood sticking out of her head, she would ignore it and worry about her hair and nails instead.

He was right.

Sex was a fix-all for Marion but Ron didn't fall for it. It was a good thing he was smarter than her or they both would end up in trouble. Instead he protected her.

"That's all right baby."

Ron wrapped his arms around her and held on tight. She was like a little girl sometimes, always trying to please and looking for approval. And hardly ever serious.

She was so pretty and helpless right now. He loved her so much.

The career she sought wasn't just to sustain her—she had finances. Ron thought Marion was losing her grip on reality.

She would sit day after day and either watch news, work on her little radio show or try to engage him in conversation about his day, his plans. He didn't even want to talk to her anymore. He saw her in a different light. She had her money and she was content. She didn't have many friends, wasn't very social and put her children in an exclusive boarding school that guaranteed her being there would to lead to Ivy

League colleges and beyond. It was if she was done. Done living and set on auto pilot except that she hadn't yet lived or loved or grown. She was like a teenager almost living in a world devoid of anything she didn't like and some of the things she did like.

Marion had even stopped shopping. She put a few pieces in the home and that was it. She didn't interior design like the other women Ron had known—even his own mother—who had little but seem to make it out to be a lot.

"Baby, be honest with me. Do you miss your career or do you plan to do this— what you are doing—which is basically nothing? You put your kids in prep school and you fiddle with this Internet radio thing and that's it. You don't even shop anymore. What's wrong, baby?"

Marion was numb. She was so numb that Ron's words seemed far away. She didn't have an answer. She sobbed. She made herself cry.

"I don't know."

Marion was always afraid to cry because she was scared she wouldn't stop. She didn't want her kids to see her so fragile. She felt stupid most of the time. She knew not to validate her feelings aloud but the thoughts were always there.

Sex with Ron killed those thoughts. The time spent going out, shopping, drinking, hanging out with friends helped but anything can get old and stop working effectively. Friends have their own lives—even Ron. He had been busy lately.

Why buy clothes when you don't wear them? There were scores of unworn dresses, pant suits, skirt sets--hanging tag-on--in her closet. She stopped pushing unworn clothing into her closet months ago. It seemed so pointless. The clothes didn't help her feel better about herself anymore. She wasn't special.

Ron was scared. He felt responsible for her and she seemed to be disintegrating into someone he had not yet gotten to fully know.

"Hey, let's go away for a while. I've been thinking about it and we've never vacationed together," Ron said, kissing her on the forehead.

Marion was happily stunned. Maybe that is all she needed some time off from her life. She hadn't had a vacation in years. The vacation she was supposed to have, turned into a life-changing move to Florida and it had been stressful.

"Hey, that is a great idea. Let's take the kids too, okay?"

Okay. Where will we go?" Europe? Spain?"

"Europe. It seems like a relaxing place for family get-a-ways. "Do you have a passport?

"No, do you?

"No and neither do the kids.

"Hmmm. Well, let me make some calls—see how many friends I still have. After we know when we'll get the passports, we can set a date for the trip."

"We're going to Europe then."

Marion was silent for a while. She snuggled her face into his chest.

"I feel better already, Ron. Thanks,"

"We'll soon be husband and wife. That's what I'm here for—to save you, take care of you," he said.

Ron kissed her deeply and ran his strong hands across her breasts. He wanted to make love to her. She was so sweet and innocent in her love for him. She was soft, pampered. He turned her on, he knew it. She softly raked her teeth against his neck ending in a kiss using her moist lips and tongue. He wanted her so much his face went hot and he felt heady. The lovers moved to the bedroom and onto the bed into ecstasy. He felt their lovemaking was like music.

Ron surprised Marion with a spring wedding in France.

Everyone she knew was there. In retrospect, she was glad she had friends and family with money. It wasn't all for naught, as she was beginning to think.

Marion, Ron, Nicey, Nicey's husband, Bobby, Marion's children, her parents, their friends and Ron's coworkers, parents and friends, enjoyed the celebration tucked away within the French countryside.

CHAPTER 15
GAS STATION DIVAS

The gas station divas, as Marion took to calling them, seethed. Francis and Sherry heard through other police, who stopped in at the gas station for free car washes, accidently on purpose let the cat out of the bag. Mostly just to get a reaction.

Francis had taken to wearing more eye makeup than usual. She got the idea from a celebrity trend at the time. Of course, Sherry followed suit. Both of them--false eye lashes, dark blue eye shadow and kohl liner--the complete smoky eye, handed out Speedy Reward Cards and rang up gas, schlepped garbage and cleaned grills. They even modified their smocks when the manager wasn't looking. Both women garnered their own fans--men who went out of their way to buy from that station because of the spectacle the women made of themselves. They worked and seethed. They and their teen pregnancies, afternoon drama and ridiculous pecking order at a gas station mini-mart, continued.

Francis was hurt. She couldn't understand how Ron could show her so much attention--as if he liked her--and then act as if she didn't exist. It was as if she was just something for him to do until he met the woman he really wanted. She couldn't figure out what was different about her that would have him pick Marion--who was older, plainer, ditzier and out-of-touch, over her as a wife.

"What's wrong Francis?"

She hunched her shoulders.

"Nothing."

Sherry looked at her friend for a moment. They had been working their way up the proverbial gas station chain of command for the past five years. She knew when Francis was upset. She left her alone. She could be mean when she was upset.

Sherry went about re-stocking the refrigerated case with beverages.

Francis, noticing the store was quiet, cleaned the grill and replaced the items.

She enjoyed her work when the store was quiet. She could think but at the same time, concentrate on something simple like the grill. Her mind could wonder and figure out what was going on.

She went to the cooler to get more hot dogs.

"What is wrong with me?" Francis asked Sherry, her eyes tired and caked from the weight of the cheap drug store lashes and old eyeliner she dug out of her purse.

Sherry looked at her.

"Nothing is wrong with you. Why are you letting this wedding in France thing get to you? It is so MTV."

"Why would he not marry me. Why not ask me?" Francis said, pointing at her own self.

"I work, take care of my babies--I don't waste money--like *her...*"

Francis' voice seemed as tired as her face. Marion, compared to Francis, was a pure as the driven snow. Simple taste, understated, hard to get.

"I would not have taken Ron as the type of man who would choose a woman based on how much money she has. That is the only real difference between us. I just really would not have figured him to be that way. I wouldn't have fooled with him had I known."

"I don't think it's that Francis. I think Marion went to college and got married or something--you know, *that* type of woman."

Oh, the type of woman who looks down her nose at women like me? Like you? So, what I was a teen mother! That was a long time ago. I worked my way up to this position, shift supervisor. I didn't keep having babies and even if I did so what? As long as I am taking care of myself and my children who should say how many I have?

"Well, it's just that Ron went to college too, didn't he?"

"Yeah, I guess. We really didn't talk about that kind of thing. I rocked his world! There was nothing that we didn't do. And he has a baby's momma too!"

"Girl, he was married to her,"" Sherry said, turning back to her work. She was getting tired of Francis'' temper tantrums and the subsequent psychoanalysis of what was real and what was not real.

Sherry remembered the day she told her mother she was pregnant. She really didn't have to tell. She had begun to show and she couldn't comfortably hold it in any longer. That was the day the whole world turned a deaf ear to her. No one talked to her anymore--they just looked at her stomach.

It was met with silence and eyes averted. She knew her mom had wanted her to go to college. Her parents had been saving a little bit each month for years. They used it to get her an apartment, a car and stuff for the baby. They had planned a wedding but Carl didn't show up and no one would tell them where he had moved.

Gas Station Divas

His parents wouldn't talk to Sherry or her parents at all. They stopped getting invites, there was no cotillion to plan for, no scholarships--nothing.

She went to night school to finish her high school diploma and then found a job. That had been her life for the past five years. She was numb from the daily monotony. She watched television until she fell asleep after picking her daughter up from daycare. Her parents refused to watch her. They were both ostracized and humiliated but constantly trying to work their way back into the good graces of society.

Sherry's sister graduated with honors and was granted a scholarship to an Ivy League school. She remembers the look on her parent's faces at the graduation. She could see the pride in their faces. They didn't say anything to her. They went out to dinner and everyone cooed over how cute their granddaughter Sarah was with the waitress and how well she was doing--in spite of her dumb ass mother. That was always the unspoken part of the compliment. Sherry was a loser in their eyes--damaged goods. She didn't see why Francis didn't understand that and why she was always thinking her way was good, okay and acceptable. People had not much changed their minds about unwed teen mothers since the 1950s except that they no longer made the girl put her baby up for adoption or necessarily shunned her.

Instead of a point of shame and ridicule, they became invisible--an invisible new underclass of people who took service industry jobs for minimum wage and worked them. The waitresses, laundry room attendants, cashiers and the gas station divas. Important in their own right to them and themselves only. Clowns to everyone else. There was no brighter day for them. They were considered stupid and pathetic. They weren't to marry decent guys like Ron--a cop-- they were practice girls, jump-offs and good-time girls--not wives.

Tears began to well up in Sherry's eyes. She was tired of her life, sorry she had sex in high school and sorry she got pregnant. She never had any money to spend on anything except an occasional lipstick and she had been thinking lately of becoming a stripper.

She met a few who frequented the gas station and they always told her how cute she was and how tight her body was. They had been teen mothers too and their mothers, even.

One girl said she and her mother actually got pregnant at the same time by the same man! Her mom blackmailed him and they ended up getting a double wide out of the deal. Sherry actually stopped crying at that thought because she had started laughing. It was so fucking ridiculous and at least she wasn't that pathetic. The girl came in drunk one night and began telling her the same story again and let it slip that she thought her mom set it up that way, so that she could get him over a barrel.

"What in the hell are you laughing at? Me?" Francis said, box cutter in hand.

Gas Station Divas

"Naw, girl--I was just thinking about what that one stripper said about how she got pregnant and her mom set her up," Sherry said.

"Oh, the drunk stripper?"

"Yeah."

The cooler fell silent but for the sound of boxes frozen hot dogs, heavy bottles and cans being slung, moved, cut open and stacked about.

"Yeah, that is kinda fucked up."

Francis and Sherry looked at the floor of the cooler in silence, sucking their teeth and shaking their heads in disbelief. Francis let a chuckle slip out.

"Damn, that is fucked up."

The women laughed for the first time that day because at least they were not that pathetic.

Francis, feeling herself-- her roaring woman-ness move over her--head tossed her teased bouffant out of her face.

"His dick was kinda small anyway. I just worked with it really good," she remarked.

Sherry put her hands up to her face laughing and embarrassed.

"You are a fool! Girl, what is wrong with you?"

Francis laughing, carrying out boxes of frozen hot dogs, hunched her shoulders.

"I don't know girl. Fuck it. That bitch probably didn't give him none before they got married anyway. That's her surprise to deal with. On top of that, Imma fuck one of his cop friends," Francis said. The women did a low-five side slap and strutted out of the cooler--raucous laughter and female shit-talking filling the empty convivence mart.

Gas Station Divas

Chapter 16   Send in the Clowns

Marion's wedding in France was of storybook lore. Guests left for home the next day which left the newlyweds to Paris and love. Ron noticed his phone had been strangely quiet so when it rang with Francine's text message, he noticed. She expressed her displeasure with the off-putting news of his nuptials. He didn't care for her message or tone but he didn't expect any different from her. Marion's reaction was another matter. He was her husband and he felt she should trust him enough to not go through his Blackberry.

More disturbingly, she went through the Blackberry after a session of hot honeymoon sex, effectively ending the honeymoon. He had to be more careful of his newly nosey wife.

Ron chose to enjoy the Parisian atmosphere rather than start their first official argument.

Marion's face was hot. She was embarrassed at the thought she had found a man to be true to her. She furiously packed enough things to get her home and arranged for the trunks to be shipped to her home.

She felt like Carrie on Sex in the City when her Russian boyfriend accidently slapped the shit out of her; accept she didn't have a Mr. Big--in her mind anyway.

The cool rain-fresh air hit her face and she began to run to the metro. She ticked off all of the things she needed to do before leaving her new husband. The kids went back with her parents—they were safe. She had her things shipped home—gifts included and she left Ron's things as they were—scattered about the room. Fuck him. She never wanted to be put in a position to *need* a man. This situation was one painful reason why.

It didn't hurt to leave looking fabulous. She was dressed like a runway model in heels, leggings and a bubble dress and turned many heads on the way to board the Monorail to wherever it was she was going. Even she didn't know where she was going but it had to be first class. She told herself she would get off the train at the last stop. She ended up in Spain.

Marion de-boarded and found a hotel room, undressed, got into bed and cried herself to sleep. When she awoke the next morning, she looked like heck. Her eyes were puffy and swollen and crusted with old tears. She saw that the hotel had a spa and she took full advantage of it. Six hours later, she looked more fabulous that she did on her wedding day but she felt like crap inside.

She took a seat at a bistro and enjoyed the weather. Her clothing didn't hold back and she was noticed. The Durable Medical Company's owner and master planner's assistant Andros saw her. He immediately called his boss.

84

"Yes, can you believe, Marion is here in Madrid. She is so beautiful. She seems to be glowing. Do you want me to bring her to you?"

"Yes, and thank you my dear friend. Yes, bring her to me. I knew that marriage would not last."

"Yes, I will send her by limo to the boat. Okay? Yes?"

"Yes. How will you get her to go with you?"

"I know how, believe me. I am Andros."

"Awww. You are my friend but she will not go with *you*."

"Let's wager. Next week I go on holiday with a 400000-euro bonus if she goes with me. Yes?

"Yes, but no raise will be issued next year if she does not go with you. Yes?"

"Deal, Boss."

Andros had already spent the more than $500,000 dollars in his mind.

He had champagne sent to Marion and turned on the European charm. He looked as if his face had been chiseled out of marble and his cock was hard.

Marion looked up from her drink and was stunned. They talked for three hours. He called for a limo from the table and Marion willingly climbed inside. Andros even sent for her things from the hotel and had them ready for her at the yacht.

She thought it was his at first but upon close inspection, she recognized the name. She was so young—just a college student when she met Melos Carville. They met through a dating web site and he took her to California for spring break along with seven of her closest friends. A man overdosed at a party and Melos sent them back home immediately on his private jet. None of the women ever brought it up and didn't think much of it as they continued their spring break festivities at Fort Lauderdale with the rest of the college students. Marion remembered he didn't much call after the Incident and she decided to let sleeping dogs lie.

She turned to look at Andros who had been by her side. He had slipped away and she could see him de-boarding the boat. Her heart started to race. What had she done?

She walked away with a charming stranger and now she was on Milo's boat.

"Hello Marion. You look well," Melos said.

He had appeared from nowhere with two beautiful women in tow. One of them handed her a glass of champagne.

Melos hugged her. She was stunned.

"I haven't seen you in over 15 years!" How or what..."

Marion stood there, stumbling to find the right words as Melos laughed.

"Andros saw you at the bistro and I asked him to bring you here. What, you thought this was his boat?"

"No. Ahhh yes, I did actually. Well, how the hell are you?

Melos and the women laughed and led Marion to the deck of the yacht. They drank the night away. When Marion awoke, she was in her own cabin, her things by her side and dressed in a gold metallic string bikini complete with stiletto heels. Melos always did have great taste but she did not savor the fact she had no memory of changing.

"Well sleepyhead, glad to have you join us!"

Dressed in white, the trio was enjoying breakfast. Goat cheese, grapes, olives—very Mediterranean. She took a seat.

"What time is it?" Marion said.

"Well, you've been asleep for two days, what time do you need it to be?"

Marion thought she would only leave her husband for a day and return home. Here she was on a yacht in the middle of whatever ocean in a gold bikini feeing both woozy and satisfied. Her whole body was smooth and slippery. She had no idea what had happened. A servant brought a place setting and some espresso. She requested cream and sugar and it was placed on the table with a sniff. The women were excused by Melos.

"You know dear, we did not give you that money to waste traipsing around Europe," Melos said.

Marion stared at the silver fox. His eyes were as blue as the ocean and stood out against his weathered, burnished skin. He looked like the senior version of the Marlboro Man.

"What money?" Marion said coyly. She figured how he could know and that he was just fishing.

"Durable Medical Supply is one of my companies. I told them to hire you there after you left the newspaper."

"How did you know about that? The newspaper?"

"Let's just say I wanted to keep in touch with you but after that idiot and the party ... well I did not want you and your friends involved in such things."

Marion stared blankly and felt lost.

"You spied on me?"

"No not *you* per say but I had some people ask about you. I kept up. You were such a beautiful and smart girl. I wanted to see you do well in life. You were a good reporter but everything comes to an end. I had someone send you that offer to work at Durable Medical. You never applied for the position."

"Yeah, I remember that. I thought that I just forgot applying or something. I had gone to every job fair in the Tri-State area then I got that correspondence. I didn't ask questions. I needed a job then. Thank you, Melos. How generous of you," Marion said, landing a kiss on his cheek and a hug around the neck.

"Thank you, Melos. That job was my saving grace."

Gas Station Divas

Marion's eyes welled up with tears. The memories flooded her. Crying in the hot sun, reflected off of the Bay of Biscay, Marion realized what a dumb mistake she had made. She told Melos everything; however, he had grown tired of her. She was not the happy co-ed he had met so long ago. She was a woman who had become a mess in spite of the help he had extended to her. He didn't understand why she was not smiling and happy and told her such.

"I just need a little air, Melos."

"You are in the middle of the sea, the ocean. If you cannot get air here, I don't know where you can get it," Melos said with a hearty laugh. Marion began to laugh at herself as well. The trio partied well into the night before heading back to France.

"Oh, I just left France, Marion said the next day at breakfast. The Mediterranean sun had baked her skin to deep ebony and put light streaks in her hair. The yacht was so huge that she was able to do many things while on board, including get her mojo back. She asked Melos to steer the boat towards the Gulf of Mexico because she wanted to visit her old stomping ground.

Marion was the hit of the party. She strutted around, flirting with any man available and this, Melos did not like. They argued and Marion got drunker and higher by the day.

When she awoke, she was no longer on the yacht. Instead, after she passed out, Melos had her removed from his yacht and placed in a lifeboat. She awoke and panicked. All of her things and the things Melos had given her on the boat were packed were packed and ready to go.

She climbed out and saw she was in the middle of the Atlantic Ocean. The boat had gone nowhere near the coast of Florida. Marion fainted.

When she awoke, it was night. She used a radio he had placed in the lifeboat to call for help. She actually said "mayday." The man who heard her laughed. Melos put her out there to teach her a lesson but he did not leave her alone. He put one of his ships on alert for a pretty black girl floating in the middle of the ocean and they finally rescued her by morning.

She climbed aboard the container ship as belle of the ball, dressed in a bikini and heels with her gear in tow. They, in turn dropped her at the Port of Indiana. She slept in the captain's cabin the entire time with her food brought to her by a shipmate. No one spoke to her beyond what they had to say but she could hear the laughter and the talk in foreign languages and figured she was the butt of the joke.

Marion used her cell phone to call for a cab at the port and had it take her to the airport. She flew home in heels and a coat, still looking fabulous but all the wiser for her travels.

She was back in the same situation but now she had to explain where she had been for the past two weeks to her new husband--and who was Melos. It all sounded made up.

Gas Station Divas

When she arrived home, there were several UPS stickers on her door, mail piled up inside and no Ron.

She figured he was either in Europe or had decided to move out.

She checked the voice mail. It was jammed with messages for her from Ron, her parents and her friends who had no idea where she had run off to in her anger. What would she tell them? The truth?

Ron had everyone looking for her and apparently an eye on the house. The phone rang with a very angry man on the other end. He was at work and had been staying at one of his properties. He cussed her out and called her names for 20 minutes. Marion had no defense so she took it like a woman. Then she remembered why she got mad in the first place.

"So how is Francine? Didja go see ya ho at the gas station?" Marion said, neck a-waggle.

"What, gat dammit?" Ron's flat regional twang rang out angrily.

Ron had forgotten how the whole thing started. However, what Marion did far outweighed his perceived indiscretion.

"You heard me. I checked your messages and packed my grip. You don't need me and some other woman."

There was a stony silence between them.

"What could I do? She called me!"

"Why does she have your number?"

"Look girl, I called her and told her ... what else could I do? She is in the past. You are supposed to be my future. Where did you go? Where have you been?"

"I took the Monorail to Spain. That's all."

"I called the hotels in Spain and France. There was no you registered."

Marion was silent.

"I used another name, Ron. Look, come home and let's get this unraveled. I guess I had PMS."

"Damn. Whatever." Ron hung up hotter than a cat on a tin roof.

"Lying bitch!" He screamed as he jerked the steering wheel of his squad car around in a violent U-turn.

He pulled over a speeder and gave them the ticket of a lifetime. The driver threw Ron the finger as he pulled away. Ron laughed in anger as he sped off past the driver.

Marion hung up not knowing anything. She didn't know if their conversation meant she still had a husband or not or if she still had to explain her whereabouts. She had no clue about her husband but understood his anger.

He didn't come home that night. Marion called Nicey, crying. She knew she needed help with this one.

Marion turned on the air and took a long, hot shower. She couldn't believe the mess she had started for herself.

Gas Station Divas

Ron called his friends at the Agency and told them what happened. They laughed.

"I told you dude. I don't know a woman who would have told the truth about that. It doesn't even sound believable. I wouldn't believe my woman if she told me that shit, dude," Barry, Ron's overseas connection said.

"Well you don't have a woman so shut it."

"Well, for the past two weeks, you didn't either," Barry said with a laugh.

"Later, Ron. It will work out. It's not like you can tell her how you know what you know."

"Yeah."

Ron hung up. He was stuck. Marion could never hear how her new husband was a Central Intelligence Agency operative or how he knew and had been following Melos for the past 20 years and her for the past 15 or how his name wasn't Ron and their marriage was just work—but now it wasn't--or that he knew exactly where she was every minute they are apart. Good thing she didn't switch out her weave or her tips or she would have been lost. Ron had been leaving much to chance lately.

He got to thinking about when he was given the assignment. Melos had been quietly setting up front companies across the globe for years. It was a place that foreign operatives could go for cover. When a kill order was issued on the Russian double agent at that California party Marion and her friends had attended, Ron was called in to monitor the situation. The Agency wanted to figure out what Melos' long-range plans were. They knew about the contraband but it wasn't Melos' operation nor did he benefit from it. He saw what Melos did for Marion. He actually helped her. They could not see a direct line from Melos to anyone. Other operatives were assigned to follow those who sought cover from his companies. They had international lines of connection from adversaries to allies. His job was to watch Melos and now Marion—his wife. The Agency promoted him after he married her. It showed dedication to deep cover ops and the Agency. They knew he had no way out so it was funny to them when Marion ran off and Melos found her. He too, always knew where Marion was and he was disappointed at her choice in men. Ron was just a cop as far as he knew and Melos didn't have much respect for the law.

Ron parked his squad towards the beach and tuned into the chatter going on in the house. The sounds of the ocean seemed to calm him down. Those DEA bugs came in handy when he wanted to tune into what Marion was thinking because he couldn't always tell and she was good at hiding her feelings.

He let his mind drift to when they met at that bar and how they ended up in the hot tub. He had wanted Marion to suck him off while they let the bubbles relax their muscles. He remembered how he felt when he looked at her. She was so helpless, clueless. Her face and soft breasts left his cock harder than Chinese math. Their hearts were open to each other that night.

He remembered their brief honeymoon and how much sex they had the first two days. They really connected. They made love inside and out. Marion cried with joy and Ron became weak remembering how hard he came that night. He felt dizzy and confused sitting in his squad car remembering but his pride would not let him return to their home. Marion had to learn, even if it hurt him more.

Then he thought he'd cave and be home by the weekend. Why extend his pain? Besides, he wasn't the type of man who'd walk around with his dick on hard. Why not have sex with his new bride?

CHAPTER 17
LET'S STAY TOGETHER

Marion padded through the thick shag in her bedroom and swung open her closet door. She picked a sunny colored sundress she had bought while in Indiana. It was old but rarely worn. She went braless and slipped on a white cotton thong. She felt fresh and good. She shook her hair out and ran a brush through it, topped her look off with mascara and lip gloss, grabbed her bag and walked out the door. She didn't know where she was headed but she had to go somewhere. She was so alone in the house by herself.

She headed down A1A towards Miami Beach. It was her favorite place. Breakfast was an iced Irish coffee made especially for her with lots of whipped cream and a scrape of fresh of nutmeg.

She drew the concoction deep into her throat through the straw provided. It was good and cold with just enough of a bite. She threw her head back and took a deep lung full of ocean air. There was no one on the beach and she had a clear view of the water. She settled into the silence of nature and let her mind wander. She was grateful for not having any distractions, no agenda whatsoever. She could sit there all day if she wanted and that made her happy.

Soon, she began to chuckle at herself and the antics she had just recently become involved in. She thought to herself, 'Only me. Only I could do this.' She shook her head at herself a little then picked up the phone to blather on to Nicey about her current situation.

'Where will I start so that this makes sense?' She thought to herself as the phone rang. There was no one around but her so she could talk as loudly as she wanted until the place filled up with vacationers.

Nicey was shocked at what her friend told her. It sounded like a slice of her own life.

After her conversation with her friend, Marion decided to write it all down. She went home and started a blog. She figured it would be therapeutic to write it all down to get it off of her mind. She kept her blog private and even still, her identity private. She was right; it felt good to get it out in the open, so to speak. She told her blog about how it felt to suck two cocks at once while getting fucked in the pussy. And how it felt to have several different men's' hands touch her breasts and ass. There were people coming all around her on the yacht. There were women laying inside each other's thighs to the delight of the men in the super king-sized bed. She came as watched their pink tongues lap at each clit. The women would later grind their pussies together to come again while some men stroked their cocks. They came on the women, together. Marion had Melos eat her pussy during that time. She sat on his face while one of the pretty cocktail girls rode his stiff cock and played with her nipples. His tongue was so good to her. She forgot all about her marriage. Marion came on Melos' face while watching the girl bounce wildly on his cum-filled hardness. She stopped writing for a while to reflect.

Marion was startled by the phone. It was her husband. She invited him over for coffee.

Gas Station Divas

CHAPTER 18
LUST OR LOVE

Ron looked good in his motorcycle cop gear. She made sure to look good too. She wore white boy shorts and a halter top. She was really to big up top to wear a halter without a bra but that was the point. She led her husband into the bedroom. It was ice cold inside the room. She had his favorite drink waiting, chilled and she served him. They spoke without words.

All of the writing on the blog revved up Marion's engines and Ron just wanted her back. He had tired of fucking around and Francine, he found, wasn't even worth it. She did little more than lay there until his business was done, so he felt guilty afterwards, made up an excuse and left. He didn't even like going in the convenience store anymore. He got tired of the stares and whispers.

He missed what he knew--Marion. She was sweet and kind and freaky. The house and the money didn't hurt either. It was nice that she had earned her money and didn't just get it from her parent's hard work. She was a career woman basically. She had a brain. Even if she had won the lottery, Ron found women who stayed under their parent's wing and wallet were not his cup of tea. They were bossy and assumed he'd want to marry. They didn't understand booty calls and the whole lusty dance of relationships. He found those girls got along better with men who were steeped in character flaws and only wanted them for their money. He had money and property and now he had Marion. And they fucked for hours. It would be a lie to say love making was involved. He loved her tight wetness and the way she moaned softly in his ear. It made him want to weep with joy. No other woman could match her.

They lay in repose, wet and fulfilled. Speaking no words, they stroked and nibbled themselves to sleep.

Marion had pleasant dreams that night. She went to sleep understanding that she was lucky to have the man she had. She knew what was out there. Ron, above all, was nice to her. Even when they fought, he never said the things he could have said--the hurtful things. She had seen men who had no business knowing what a practice girl was; confront a woman who could have been a loving wife to them as if she had no value at all. She had witnessed those men; tear those women down for demanding to be treated like a human being--especially after sex.

Procreation is a survival of the fittest industry and some men did not deserve to have their particular DNA reproduced. They were so mean and nasty and some were even violent. The only fault of the woman was love--misdirected love. Instead they were labeled "practice girls," and those men died alone because they were too good to marry those kinds of women. What would their friends think? If it were not for mobility, these women would die alone right along with them. Marion didn't understand how this happened, in every town and in every race, the same scenario. Some of the men were downright ugly--I-don't-have-a-hand-mirror ugly. Some were just evil and hateful toward women, so much so, it would have been better to learn they were gay. Who were they to decide a woman's fate through the label "whore" or the all-time high school favorite, "slut?" When, knowing full well, if it were not for that particular woman's kindness and soft heartedness, they would experience no type of female intimacy at all. He'd be stuck with his mate or his hand and held hostage to her whims. And, not wanting to be flexible or to bend in the face of her strength, to work things out, he would stand, frustrated when all he really wanted to do was to come and go to sleep.

So, every day, these women go unmarried and some childless. Decent good women, some born homemakers, some breadwinners but all alone, rejected and scarred.

Marion knew how good she had it and did not want to mess it up so she shelved the idea to tell Ron what happened on their honeymoon. He only needed to be concerned with the part she spent with him.

She didn't know where she was headed but she had to go somewhere. She was so alone in the house by herself. It was if Ron did not need her in his life and didn't miss her at all. Stiff and robot-y, it was if being with her was just another part of a job he performed – a job he liked but a job none the less. Everybody likes time off from their job every now and again.

She headed down A1A towards Miami Beach. It was her favorite place. Breakfast was an iced Irish coffee made especially for her with lots of whipped cream and a scrape of fresh of nutmeg.

She drew the concoction deep into her throat through the straw provided. It was good and cold with just enough of a bite. She threw her head back and took a deep lung full of ocean air. There was no one on the beach and she had a clear view of the

94

water. She settled into the silence of nature and let her mind wander. She was grateful for not having any distractions, no agenda whatsoever. She could sit there all day if she wanted and that made her happy.

Soon, she began to chuckle at herself and the antics she had just recently become involved in. She thought to herself, 'Only me. Only I could do this.' She shook her head at herself a little then picked up the phone to blather on to Nicey about her current situation.

'Where will I start so that this makes sense?' She thought to herself as the phone rang. There was no one around but her so she could talk as loudly as she wanted until the place filled up with vacationers.

Nicey was shocked at what her friend told her. It sounded like a slice of her own life – the lust-filled sex scenes fueled by whatever drug was offered. They weren't even involved in the occult, seeing as how they're known for their dark orgies and that was the shameful part. Nicey did it for her husband more than herself. She didn't want to be alone or lonely.

Marion spent her evening downloading music from Napster so that she could listen to something while driving around, looking for a job. Her session with her husband was satisfactory but he had to work so she was still alone. She thought if she could legally be paid for keeping some man's dick in her mouth, she would not have to search so hard for work. Since going to the financial planner to get her money right, Marion had been living on a strict budget funded by the interest on her money, which had trickled into a stingy lifestyle. A job would allow her to continue to recklessly spend and fulfill that hole inside her. Although she sought a high-profile job, she figured she needed media connections to get back into that life and she didn't have any.

Her CD was filled with Rufus featuring Chaka Kahn, Aaliyah, and anything else she could sing along with because she knew the words. She loved soulful music no matter the genre. And she wanted people to know what good taste she had in music. It was a conversation starter.

Marion stretched and looked around her room/office. It seemed to be time for wine. She put on something so that she could go out and get a couple bottles for Sangria. She took her new music CDs with her to the hot car. The seats were leather and could burn her after sitting out in the South Florida sunshine. She needed gas, as usual. She mused to herself that she should buy stock in the damn place as often as she was there, filling her tank but she knew better. The tank stayed three-quarters full and she still put gas in it, telling herself she was just topping it off. She was really just hoping to get a glimpse of Ron, to see if he still frequented the area and the women. She didn't need gas –her car was a remarkable gas sipper and for that, she felt ashamed of herself and pathetic.

Gas Station Divas

Dizzy from the sun or not, she picked up an application inside the convenience gas station while there took it home and filled it out, planning to return it later. Maybe it was the thick sweetness of the first few strains of the song "Intimate Friends" that led her to sit at her table, complete the app and then go back up there and turn it in. The girls behind the counter had eyes as wide as saucers. They were both shocked and afraid that women like Marion would have to apply to work were they worked. If she, driving what she drives and having what she appears to have in wealth, has to work there with them, then how much worse can the economy is for them? The young girls took the application and promptly gave it to their manager as soon as she got in. Marion went online and bought some stock in the holding company that owned the convenience gas station. She figured she shopped there enough, spent enough money there, on popcorn, hot dogs, coffee drinks, caramel corn, soda, doughnuts and the like (all to win reward points and coupons) why not? Besides, she would be in prime position to keep an eye on Ron. It is where they met and where he had met several women over the years. How many others were or could have been a wife? Did he propose to any of the women he ran across there? Even though these are questions Marion should have asked herself before she said "I Do," a woman who wanted to hold on to her man could never be too careful or too sure.

Even with all of that, she was still surprised when the manager telephoned her to schedule an interview. Marion laughed to herself at the silliness of it all and agreed to meet with her. She figured it would keep her mind off of the sadness that invaded her consciousness from time to time. She chose khakis and a polo as an interview outfit. It was the store uniform anyways.

Marion, with her hair in a bun, arrived two minutes early for the interview. One of the girls behind the counter alerted the manager and soon, she was invited into the back of the store/gas station. She didn't know what to call it besides the Quickie Mart–ala the Simpsons–and she had never seen the inner workings of such place. Inside the back of the store was dark, barely clean and stacked to the ceiling with their inventory. The manager wasn't the nice lady she had seen earlier. It was some plain girl/woman.

"Hi, Marion, I'm Uleene the district manager. I interview all of the new hires," she said with a smile. She seemed nice enough.

"Now why is it that you want to work here?"

"I need the money. I have to pay off some bills immediately," Marion heard herself lie. She never lied in an interview before because they were for corporate positions, degree required. She didn't want Uleene and the others to know her true position in life. She just wanted an outpost to watch for Ron.

Well, the hours here are around the clock because we are a 24-hour operation and there will be a training session starting on tomorrow morning at 8 a.m., can you be in attendance?" Uleene said.

"Yes, of course, ma'am. I will be there with bells on!" Marion said, not believing what she heard come from her mouth. She just hoped it all stuck.

"Great, well welcome aboard to the All-American Quick Gas-N-Stuff. We have a management trainee program that you would be wise to utilize."

Marion stuck her hand out for a quick pump up and down, out of habit and hurriedly walked out thinking if she got to her car fast enough, the woman wouldn't be able to change her mind. She couldn't believe how fast that was and how she didn't check anything in her background, Marion thought to herself. She could be anyone really but did it matter? She would later understand later why none of that mattered to the folks at the All-American Quick Gas-N-Stuff.

Marion listened to music a lot because it drowned out the sound her own brain made. Her brain was noisy and disjointed and always poked its nose it where it did not belong. It gave answers to questions not asked. It remembered too much. Marion's brain was a pain in the ass to her and she was tired of listening to it because it worried her about the wrong things. It would not focus on the things she wanted and on which she needed it to focus.

"I want to laugh but you make me want to cry. I'm tired of crying." She thought to herself as tears streamed down her face.

She made a habit of performing housework with her Mp3 player turned up as loud as it would go. That way, she wouldn't hear the phone not ring or the doorbell go unrung. The few hours she spent at her new job wasn't enough. The few times her husband paid enough attention to her to make her orgasm didn't matter anymore. Everything was coming loose. Even the children ran in then back out of her life, developing lives of their own. She couldn't cling to them anymore and it was her idea to place them in private boarding schools.

Her brain made her think of things that she couldn't discuss with others or write on her blog. The thoughts would lead others to think she was going insane. Her mantra is that she needs to stay sane for her children. She thought about all of the people in her age group and what they meant to her. She knew that many of the people who were born during her time are either still in prison or now dead--once released from prison. This is all thanks to the drug-fueled Baby Boomers whose footsteps we have since followed, she thought to herself. These people would have been vital in some way to society if nothing but to populate it. However, they are gone and this 1966 portion of Generation X will feel the gravity of it even more as we age. Those people who got addicted to crack and other drugs were to serve a greater purpose than to die young. Someone has to support this society. To hell with "do what thou whilst."

97

Gas Station Divas

That man is an idiot, she thought. I'm not an idiot. I can change. However, she was only growing up.

Gas Station Divas